OTHER BOOKS BY CHARLES AUSTIN MUIR

Bodybuilding Spider Rangers and Other Stories

Forest of Sex and Death (with Lucas Mangum and Brendan Vidito)

This Is a Horror Book

PRAISE FOR CHARLES AUSTIN MUIR'S WORK

"Charles Austin Muir is a genre unto himself. *Slippery When Metastasized* is an unrivaled blend of absurdist humor, slapstick horror, bizarro, '80s pop culture, social satire, and bittersweet literary flights of fancy laced with so much truth and untruth you won't know what you've swallowed until you're drunk to the gills with emotion. Each story is elevated by strong writing and constructed with the skill and delivery of a mad tragicomedian. If you're looking for a collection bursting with soul and mischief, look no further. Sit back and enjoy the insanity. You'll laugh your way into the abyss and maybe cry a little, too."

— BRENDAN VIDITO, WONDERLAND AWARD-WINNING AUTHOR OF *NIGHTMARES IN ECSTASY*

SLIPPERY WHEN METASTASIZED

CHARLES AUSTIN MUIR

Grateful acknowledgment is made to James J. Butler and Todd L. Duncan for permission to reprint material from their essay, "Beyond Reductionism: Bridging the Gap between Science and Meaning."

www.worldsofcharlesaustinmuir.com

Cover art/design by Don Noble

Bench Press logo by John Humphrey

Internal illustrations by Kara Muir

Internal Formatting by Sam Richard

Print ISBN# 978-1-7349346-0-1

Ebook ISBN# 978-1-7349346-1-8

CONTENTS

PREVIOUSLY PUBLISHED

"Before the Def Leppard *Pyromania* Virus Destroyed Us," *Horror Sleaze Trash* (2019)

"Smoke Nurse," *M-Brane SF #17* (2010)

"The Time I Took Hamlet Right into the Danger Zone," *Horror Sleaze Trash* (2019)

"Jim Morrison Library Poem," *Horror Sleaze Trash* (2019)

"Ding-Dong-Ditch," *Whispers of Wickedness #15* (2007)

"Insidious in the Month of June," *Byzarium #1* (2005)

ACKNOWLEDGMENTS

Thanks to the following for their contributions to my writing, mental health, and in some cases financial survival:

Kara: I can't imagine a better partner to accompany me through this journey into the dark regions.

The Freddy's Crew: Sam Richard (*THANK YOU for all the hand-holding through this project!*), Brendan Vidito, Josie Muller (Jo Quenell), and Mark Zirbel. Many, many, many binkies to you all.

My air guitar family: Jason and Lisa Farnan, Jaime Farnan, Rob Messel, Jacque Messel, Rachelle Landreth and Nielsen Nacis, John Humphrey and Rachel Sinclair, ATC "West," the U.S. Air Guitar "committee"… so many of you, too many to list, be excellent, be stupid, rock on.

My writing family: Lucas Mangum, S.C. Burke, Christoph Paul, Leza Cantoral, Maxwell Bauman, Eric Miller, C. Courtney Joyner, Shane Bitterling, S.G. Murphy, John Wayne Comunale, Scott Cole, Peter Dale, Christopher Lesko, Robert Brouhard, Don Noble, Jason Rizos, Christopher Nelson, Zé Burns, Leigham Shardlow, Kelly Dunn,

Stephen Woodworth, Jennie Komp, Anthony Rivera, Sharon Lawson, Weirdpunk, APB… so many of you, too, I'm sorry I can't list you all.

My Third Way family: Dr. Judith Boothby, DC and Catherine Klebl. You gave me one of the best jobs I've ever had and provided critical support during Kara's first cancer treatments.

Jennifer "Snake" Pliska: For everything from amazing gifts to Hawaii vacays to much-needed phone calls to deciphering scary medical jargon.

Jackie Mitchell: I'm grateful to Brian for bringing me into the lives of some of his closest friends. I feel like we've known each other a lot longer than two years… so glad Sam nudged me into buying a ticket for KillerCon.

John Dover: Scotch, writing advice, meal deliveries, karaoke, mad thespian skills, musical scores on a minute's notice… you've thrown me a lifeline so many times.

Lenny Gotter: Books. Photo shoots. Karaoke. Endless free music and movies. Kind words. Work. TCB.

David Tircuit: I don't know how I could navigate the madness of cancer, loss, and global chaos without your guidance.

James Butler: I'm so glad we are finally collaborating on fun, silly projects after knowing each other for over forty years. Tell Mini Evel I'm thankful for him, too!

Uncle Mark: Thank you for checking in on Kara and me and supporting our goofball adventures.

Mom, Dad, Brian, Aunt Dede: To quote the immortal 2Pac, "God bless the dead."

Team Picante: All you family, friends, and healthcare professionals who lift Kara up by believing in her, caring for her and reminding us both that there are those in the world who are not out to crush us.

Iggy Sancho: I miss you hard, little buddy. You were the hero of the pack. You were the best to us.

To everyone who has ever supported my writing —*thank you.*

INTRODUCTION

EXTRA LONG RANTING EDITION

On May 20, 2019, the thirtieth anniversary of my first date with the girl I would later marry, I drove Kara to a clinic for a colonoscopy and learned she had a "cancerous mass" in her rectum. The next day, I came home from work and found out the cancer had spread to both lobes of her liver.

Welcome to Hell.

At the time, I had been preparing to write a horror novel about a protagonist with parasites in his muscle tissue. Kara's diagnosis knocked the story right out of me. Like an extreme horror novel, my life had turned from an ordeal with a monster (that's another story) to a struggle against an even more savage and sadistic monster.

So, with Kara, I mobilized our resources to confront the shittier monster. In the process, the literary and philosophical themes of darkness, the abyss, the negation of meaning, the hopelessness of existence, burden of consciousness, existential pain, so many of the selling points for contemporary fiction blasting on my fellow authors' social media feeds, became, in my mind, logistical concerns (will there be hot coffee in the infusion room?) or luxurious abstractions blown up by people who were not terrified of what a doctor would say about a CT scan the next day.

Dark fiction? Edgy? Tragic? Nihilistic? Sure. Some of you mean it and nail it (don't get me wrong, *Journey to the End of the Night* is one of my favorite novels), but some of you are turning pessimistic philosophy into a soap opera. Me, I'm off for work and then to visit my wife during her first chemotherapy treatment on my birthday. Darkity-dark-dark-dark!

Anyway, in the weeks after my wife's diagnosis, I thought about writing a book about how to work out when it feels like the universe is crushing you, but then realized I wanted, maybe needed, to write more fiction. Short fiction, even though I'd put out two collections previously.

I already had a few stories written. Add to that starting point a reunion with Sam Richard, Brendan Vidito, Josie Muller (Jo Quenell), and Mark Zirbel at KillerCon outside of Austin, Texas, and the resulting hilariously fucked-up ideas (thanks, Josie, for confusing Viggo Mortensen with Liam Neeson!) that emerged from that weekend, and I felt primed to write more absurd, surreal, meta, pop-culture-laced, sentimental, satirical short pieces for a third book I decided to publish myself.

And as the collection took shape, I remembered I'd written some older stories that might fit in as well. These had been published in small press magazines that had fallen out of print many years ago. So I reread them. They differed in tone and style from the new material, but they called to me as far as changing up the feel and showing a different side of how I treat themes like death and human connection. That gave me sixteen pieces of prose and poetry to evoke the reality I had been living in since the monster in my life bowed down to, or morphed into, the shittier monster.

The monster of spread… and I'm not just talking about cancer cells anymore.

Without science, of which Western medicine is a major component, we would not live the lives we do and many of us would be dead. Science makes everything in our existence possible. It follows that scientists are pretty damn important. It does not follow that scientists are the bearers of the secret knowledge, infallible and omniscient. Nor does it follow that because science has shown the universe operates from matter, nothing matters but matter. "The universe is nothing more than particles," or the reductionist view, is a narrative derived from scientific observations, it is not the object under observation. But many scientists and nonscientists say, or proceed as if, the observations and the narrative are the same thing. Anything else is just wishful thinking.

Yet, as my friend James Butler, a physicist, points out in a paper co-authored with his colleague, Todd Duncan: "Acceptance of scientific knowledge about the world does *not* require accepting this particular narrative. Other narratives are equally consistent with the scientific facts."

Scientists and medical authorities are notorious for looking at the world through a reductionist lens. But as people have become increasingly secular-minded and educated (which, totally cool in itself), the reductionist narrative has funneled down from academic and medical institutions and spread through the minds of the masses who push half-baked, distorted, oversimplified versions of that shit all over the Web by aggressively shooting down others' opinions with so-called scientific thinking and arming themselves with jargon from the philosophical and psychological fields as well. This is not about choosing a narrative about the universe that resonates with you. It is about standing out from the crowd and being right.

A reductionist narrative derived from scientific observations has become a means of correcting and dismissing others' views scaled down from a narrowly read thesis paper and skeletonized in a social media post, thread, or comment. And it's not even about the idea or argument being corrected or dismissed, but about the wit and insightfulness of the person doing the correcting or dismissing. And few can get away from this cycle, which is why I think of it as a form of spread, or… *truth cancer.*

Boom!

Even this introduction is a dismissal of dismissing. A stance on stancing. But bear with me, because I veered into this territory for a reason. The reason is this: It sucks enough watching my wife get ground up in the reductionist narrative that powers the Western medicine that we need, I watch everything from baby boomers to the latest *Star Wars* movie get cherry-picked and reduced on social media with the same rigid authority as a surgeon cutting down every question I ask as if it's an indication of some false, pathetic hope.

Could I unplug for a while? Sure, but social media is an essential part of the hustle if you're a writer. My point is that truth cancer is a mutation and disease of reductionism (which is a narrative and not necessarily harmful in itself) that spreads and spreads.

Truth cancer is crazy.

Real cancer is crazy.

A group of viruses spreading all over the world is crazy.

Having all three be part of your normal day is crazy.

I'm crazy.

But I'm less crazy, I want to think, for having written this book.

This hopefully fun, weird, sometimes sad, but not so darkity-dark-dark book.

It won't be to everyone's tastes. It certainly won't appeal to the reader who demands a strictly "transparent" writing style, one that never calls attention to the text itself or to the elements of fiction. It may disappoint or even annoy the reader who thinks that pop culture references damage a story's literary or instructive potential, regardless of how they are deployed.

If you are the reader who hates being reminded that someone is telling you a story from time to time (wink wink, nudge nudge—grrrrr!), you won't like this book. If you are the reader who thinks identifying a trope or technique is always the same as being distracted by a poorly executed trope or technique (ugh, I spotted some backstory in the dialogue—William Gibson, you suck!), you won't like this book.

But if you're willing to be different readers to different layers of relation between author and narrator, if you're open to inversions, intrusions, reifications, and other experiments that sound fancy but are mostly pretty dumb at heart—in addition to more conventionally told stories, maybe you will find something to enjoy in my attempt to cope with the ups and downs of supporting a loved one who is dealing with cancer before and during a pandemic.

Charles Austin Muir

AIR GUITAR POEM THAT NEVER ONCE MENTIONS BON JOVI

For Kara "Picante" Muir

You are my air guitar.
I was born to play you.
We rock the stage together.

And yet somehow
a tumor has grown
inside our music.

This meeting
with the oncologist
will be hard.

It will feel like
the audience hated our
imitation of real rock stars.

It will feel like
being told we lagged

behind the beat too much.

But I think
we look great.
Even now.

Your airness, my fingers
still pumping out power
ballads after all these years,

(I'll be there for you
these five words I swear
to you)

even if the latest song
stings like wicked ointment,
even if the solo
sets the stage on fire.

SLIPPERY WHEN METASTASIZED

THE DAY BEFORE HIS FORTY-FIRST BIRTHDAY, MY FRIEND learned he had cancer. The news shook him so badly he handed me the phone.

"I'm sorry to say the condition is aggressive," the gastroenterologist told me. "I've put through a request for your friend to come back as soon as possible."

"Is it… far along?"

"Well, it sure looks that way. I'll have to transfer you to the oncology department."

I waited for the call to go through.

"Bad Medicine Clinic," the receptionist said. "What is your date of birth, please?"

"This isn't for me," I said. "I'm calling for a friend."

"What is their date of birth, then?"

"We don't know. We made one up so we could celebrate it."

"It doesn't have to be exact."

"Sometime in 1977."

"Sometime in 1977…" The receptionist put me on hold.

I waited to the music of Search Warrant's 1989 power ballad, "Paradise."

She came back on while I sang along to the chorus, *Para-dise is sooooo nearrrrrrr…*

"Okay," she said, "your friend is scheduled to see Dr. Ligotti Bongiovi tomorrow at 2 p.m. Will you be accompanying him?"

"Yes. Did you say… Ligotti Bongiovi?"

"*Doctor* Ligotti Bongiovi. Why? Have you heard of him?"

"No… I don't think so."

"Dr. Ligotti Bongiovi is our founder and the only triagnostician in the world who specializes in cancer treatment. You're very fortunate he's available."

"But doesn't my friend need to see a doctor? What is a triagnostician?"

"You'll find out at the appointment tomorrow. I'm going to send you to the business department to discuss your payment plan."

"But—"

"Nebulous Institute of Esoteric Healing Sciences Business Department. What is your date of birth, please?"

Dr. Ligotti Bongiovi. Why did the name sound vaguely familiar? I looked him up online.

According to the Nebulous Institute of Esoteric Healing Sciences's website, Dr. Ligotti Bongiovi "has a medical degree and doctoral degrees in philosophy, creative writing, and musicology as well as board certifications in medical oncology, oncological ontology, epistemological hematology, musicological immunology, immunological nihilism, gastroenterological composition, clinical obfuscation, and musico-cervical hyperextension pathology."

When not treating patients, the cancer expert could be seen "touring with his high-octane rock'n'roll band, Ligotti Bongiovi, except during periods of anhedonia (inability to feel pleasure) and severe panic-anxiety."

In addition to founding the Bad Medicine Clinic and rocking concert halls since the 1980s, Dr. Ligotti Bongiovi authored a highly lauded horror-fiction collection, *Slippery When Metastasized*.

"Wow, this guy is well-rounded," I told my friend. "Not your usual specialist. Looks like you're in good hands."

My friend sparkled as he always did—though I could tell he had qualms about our appointment.

"Hey, man," I said, "I know you're scared. But let's give this Dr. Ligotti Bongiovi a shot. He wrote a song called 'I'll Be Around When You Need Me' back in the Eighties. I've never heard of him, but that doesn't mean he's not legit. Just think… you might be getting chemo from a rock star!"

Slippery When Metastasized cost a small fortune in the rare book market, but most of Ligotti Bongiovi's albums were free on the Internet. We listened to the band's *Maximum Greatest Hits* album on the way to the Bad Medicine Clinic.

"*Puuuuuuuut your gloves on me-uh, puuuuuuuut your gloves on me-uh…*" I sang along to one of the best power ballads I had ever heard. Arguably better than Sundree Gäng's 1985 rock anthem, "Great To Be Home."

Judging by his sparkliness in the passenger seat, even my friend felt uplifted by the track's manly harmonies and driving beat. Once we got out of the car though, his spirits sank to the miserable level that had kept him awake all night. Not that anyone could have told that when we stepped through the revolving doors into the chilly lobby of the Nebulous Institute of Esoteric Healing Sciences.

The receptionist waved us over.

"Perfect timing." She put down her bag of cheese puffs and rubbed her hands together. "You're here for the children's party in the Center for Teleological Pediatrics, right?"

"We're here to see Dr. Ligotti Bongiovi."

"Oh, really? I would've sworn… huh. Okay. Which of you is the patient, then?"

"My friend."

"You sure look like the entertainer we hired for the children's party." The receptionist tapped her orange-dusted forefinger in the air in a flirty gesture toward my friend. "Date of birth, please?"

"Sometime in 1977."

"Can't your friend speak?"

"That's problematic."

"Sorry. Okay, hang a right at the end of the hall, a left at the Existential Breast Cancer Monument, another left at the Monistic Meditation Room, a right at the Cancer Bistro, then take the purple elevator to the eleventh floor of the Bad Medicine Clinic. Need a map?"

The folding map had cheese puff dust on it.

"I think we've got it, thanks."

The receptionist's directions were spot on. Right outside the Cancer Bistro, I stopped at a restroom. While relieving myself, I read a flyer on the wall about a fundraiser for the Center for Teleological Pediatrics—culminating in the party whose entertainer resembled my friend.

Then I saw a sign next to the paper towel dispenser. It said: *"You have the right to ask all staff members if they washed their hands after going to the bathroom last."*

A balding man in a three-piece suit walked in.

"Welcome to the crazy world of cancer," he said. He ducked into the handicapped stall.

"Excuse me?"

"Come around here enough and you won't even notice those signs anymore."

The conversation ended in pooping noises.

My friend and I rode the purple elevator to the eleventh floor of the Bad Medicine Clinic. My urge to pee again made me realize my fight-or-flight response had kicked in, triggered by information overload. After all, in the last five minutes, we had passed a sign for just about every illness and disorder associated with the human body. And here we were, checking into the department that dealt with the Godzilla of life-threatening diseases—cancer!

The man in the three-piece suit was right. The world of cancer is crazy. It's like being trapped in an airport and finding out everyone has a bomb inside them.

A childish notion, but I couldn't shake it as I glanced around the busy waiting area.

"You check in," I told my friend. "I have to pee again."

I hit the restroom around the corner from the elevators. A sign above the toilet said: *"Please flush three times."* A sign above the toilet paper roll said: *"You have the right to ask all staff members if they put on clean underwear this morning."* And a sign next to the paper towel dispenser said: *"You have the right to ask all staff members if they have gotten a tattoo in the last twenty-four hours."*

I thought about the last twenty-four hours. I had spent them reassuring my friend and listening to Eighties hair metal bands. Even now, considering my pal's life was at stake, that seemed to be the best way to go forward. Because the moment we arrived at the hospital, what began as a phone call mutated into a convoluted navigation system in the heart of everyone's worst fears—a fairy-tale labyrinth full of red tape and time bombs ticking inside human bodies.

To stop the maze from swallowing us, we needed to pump ourselves up and take on the obstacle course, an obnoxious mingling of the mundane and nightmarish.

I had just zipped my pants when I felt the need to pee again.

If only my bladder would get on board.

"WHAT IS your date of birth, please?"

"Sorry, my friend has trouble speaking."

"Do you know his date of birth?"

"Sometime in 1977."

"Sometime in 1977… Okay. You're to see Dr. Ligotti Bongiovi in Room 9."

"Got it. Did you wash your hands after the last time you went to the bathroom?"

"Yes. Room 9 is down the hall and to your left."

"Did you put on clean underwear this morning?"

"Yes. Here, let me give you a visitor's pass."

"Thanks. Did you get a tattoo in the last twenty-four hours?"

"No."

"I have the right to ask you these questions."

"Dr. Ligotti Bongiovi is running a few minutes late. And yes—you do."

"Try to chill out," I told my friend in the examination room. "Dr. Ligotti Bongiovi is just here to give us information. I'll tell him we only want to hear about your treatment options, not about the prognosis. Sound good?"

My friend sparkled morosely.

Finally, after I replayed "Put Your Gloves On Me" in my head three times, the Bad Medicine Clinic's founder sauntered into the room.

Dr. Ligotti Bongiovi wore a white coat over a black V-neck sweater tucked into gray slacks. He looked trim for someone in his late fifties, although you wouldn't have guessed his age at a glance. For he had no eyes or nose. His head was a white egg shape with the hospital logo—a red fist punching forward—emblazoned above a slit that approximated a mouth.

He set his medical bag on the examination table and stared at us with hands on hips.

"Date of birth, please?"

"Sometime in 1977," I said.

"Shouldn't you two be at the children's party?"

"My friend has cancer."

"I know that."

"He's not the entertainer they hired for the party."

"It's uncanny, then."

"What?"

"The resemblance. Your friend must be A Film Strip Of

Greedo Firing First, am I right? The moment before Han Solo fires back at the bounty hunter across the table. You are familiar with *Star Wars*?"

"Of course. Would I have bought an authentic *Star Wars* film strip if I hadn't seen the movie? But you're wrong. My friend is A Film Strip Of Han Solo Firing First. I'm sure he'd be happy to let you read the ID card beneath the strip if you like."

"No, that's all right. I'm remembering now. We did hire A Film Strip Of Greedo Firing First, not one of Han Solo firing first. Good call."

Dr. Ligotti Bongiovi paced back and forth.

"Hmm, let me see if I can recall the exact difference between the two. Now, when your friend was shown onscreen in 1977, audiences heard a blaster firing and saw flash sparks of Greedo getting hit. Whereas, in the 1997 re-release, audiences heard *two* blasters firing and saw extra frames of the bounty hunter shooting first... because George Lucas wanted Han Solo to seem more gallant. Well, I think your friend is more entertaining than the film strip we hired. Your friend should go to the party."

"He has cancer."

"I know that."

"He only wants to know his treatment options. Not the prognosis."

"Let me check some numbers." Dr. Ligotti Bongiovi went to the laptop cart by the door.

While he scrolled through my friend's medical records, he licked his lips. An unnerving sight, considering he had no animating features except for the doll-like mouth.

"Doctor Ligotti Bongiovi," I said, "did you wash your hands after the last time you went to the bathroom?"

"Yes, I did. I also put on clean underwear this morning and have not gotten a tattoo in the last twenty-four hours."

"I have the right to ask you these questions."

"Of course, you do. I wrote the rule myself. Okay. I'm sorry to say your friend has stage 10 liver cancer."

"I didn't know there was a stage 10."

"There are more than twenty stages, from both clinical and surgical standpoints."

"So, he's not that far along?"

Dr. Ligotti Bongiovi went to his medical bag and pulled out a mask. When he slipped it on, he transformed from an eyeless, noseless oncologist into a dour, bespectacled man who looked as if he didn't get out much.

"Before we discuss treatment options," the glowering man said, "your friend should consider whether he *wants* to prolong his life in a frigid and desolate universe. He should ask himself whether he considers a reduction of his tumor growths to be tantamount to a reduction of his suffering."

"Uh... what?"

"There is no big picture, sir, no 'grand scheme of things.' There is no purpose to our existence, no benefit to our participation and investment in the machinery of actions that keeps us enduring one ordeal after another, day after day, grief after grief, terror after terror."

"I don't understand what this has to do with my friend's treatment options."

"The options? Your friend can add chemotherapy infusions to the horrors he has suffered ever since his brain matured enough to form an intelligible thought... or he can refuse treatment and relinquish his claim to belong to a 'grand scheme of things' in his inflammatory condition."

"So you're saying chemo is my friend's number one option?"

"Certainly… although with the caveat that this would perpetuate your friend's greater sickness: The instinct to stymie death, when in fact he could reframe the situation not as a frightening game of misbehaved cells, but rather as an opportunity for *metastatic enlightenment.*"

"I don't know, Doctor… we'll have to think about this."

Dr. Ligotti Bongiovi removed his mask and set it on the examination table. Again, he pulled a mask from his medical bag and donned it. This time, he transformed into a young man with smoldering eyes, sensuous lips, and teased hair that looked as if some ferocious critter had rolled around in toxic chemical waste.

"*Hmm…mmm…mmm…*" The young man closed his eyes and hummed up and down the major scale. I recognized the vocal warm-up from my singing lessons in middle school. I also recognized his voice—minutes before, I had heard it belting out "*Puuuuuuuut your gloves on me-uh*" in my head.

With a slight change of costume, Dr. Ligotti Bongiovi had metamorphosed into the founder and lead singer of my new favorite Eighties rock band—Ligotti Bongiovi!

"*Hope,*" he sang, "*babe, we're gonna get through this stor-rrrrrmmm… Gaawwd, we can't give up hope…*"

"That's how I feel," I said, and clapped my hands together. "Just because my friend has stage 10 cancer doesn't mean we should give up hope, right?"

"*Hope! Our love is gonna keep us waaaarrrrrrm… This tii-ime we can't give up hope…*"

"So you think the chemo will work?"

The lead singer doffed the mask, leaving my friend and I with Dr. Ligotti Bongiovi again.

"We should begin palliative care immediately," he said. "I believe the chemotherapy will be very effective. Your friend should go in for port surgery as soon as possible."

"He can go into remission, then?"

The oncologist donned the first mask again.

"In medical parlance," his somber, bespectacled replacement said, "*palliative* means we can improve and maintain your friend's quality of life for however long he responds to treatment. It does *not* refer to curing his cancer. In other words, I can shrink your friend's tumors, but I can not get rid of them completely. From what I've seen, the surgical staging suggests an even worse problem. But as far as intervention goes, you'll have to wait for a response from the Epiphenomenal Investigations Department of Malignant Tumors."

"So you're saying my friend is always going to have cancer?"

"The real question is how far your friend is willing to bear the crippling sadness of this world *compounded* by the side effects of chemotherapy. Does he wish to endure the torments of existence *and* science-based medicine? Or would he rather fade into darkness, delivered at last from the cruelties of consciousness, the vicious illusions of survival instinct?"

Mystified by the sullen man's words, my friend and I sat in silence.

Finally, Dr. Ligotti Bongiovi reappeared and brought back the lead singer of Ligotti Bongiovi.

"*Ohh-ohhhh, we're on our wayy-aayyyyy, ohh-ohhhh, ruuu-uunning on faiiiith!*"

"*Hold me tiiiiight,*" I joined in, "*today's our daaayyyyy, ohh-ohhhh, ruuuuunning on faiiiiith!*" I stood. "All right, so where do we schedule my friend's port surgery?"

WHEN WE GOT off the elevator, I had to pee again. I left the men's room knowing I had the right to ask all staff members if they had ever worn a cashmere sweater, tried water aerobics or eaten a tuna salad sandwich under a bridge next to a homeless person.

Though these announcements amused me—so random and obsessed with my rights as a hospitalgoer—I wondered when I would cease to notice them. With enough time in the labyrinth, would I go bald and wear three-piece suits?

For our next stop, my friend had to check in at the Transhumanist Surgery Center on the other end of the campus. Along our route, I asked three staff members if they had ever eaten puffer fish, written a nasty email to a loved one or participated in a Masonic orgy. They all confirmed at least one action, and none of them seemed to suspect I had made the questions up.

Halfway to the surgery center, my friend started shaking. He rushed over to a bench in front of the Ascetic Ostomy Corner. I joined him and squeezed his knee, careful not to smudge the acrylic glass framing his authentic 1977 *Star Wars* film cells.

"Come on, buddy," I said, "we're going to get through this. We'll schedule your surgery and go for cheese steaks when we're done. Anyway, your oncologist isn't so bad, is he? He just needs multiple personalities to explain what he thinks he can do for you."

My friend's sparkle lit up, a little.

"There's the doctor with the stats," I said, raising my forefinger to represent the oncologist. "Then there's the Debbie Downer who's afraid you won't make it." With my middle finger, I counted the bespectacled man, no doubt the personality who had written *Slippery When Metastasized*. "Then there's the rock star who thinks you can beat your disease if you believe in yourself." With my ring finger, I counted the only personality in the triumvirate I would want to hang out with.

"I think we should cut Dr. Ligotti Bongiovi some slack," I continued. "I mean, it can't be easy for him to talk to people all day about their tumors. Look, I have to pee again. Sit tight. Think of the oncologist as a performer… his consultations are like one-man shows that express the ideas and emotions he can't communicate as a medical practitioner. Weird, but kind of cool, right? Maybe he should be the one entertaining at the children's party!"

I let my friend ponder my multiple-personality theory. Not only did it make sense, but it also explained the occupational title, "triagnostician." As if that mattered. What mattered was that my friend could not be cured, in Dr. Ligotti Bongiovi's expert opinion. Hearing his diagnosis, supposing I'd been an authentic *Star Wars* film strip like my friend, I would have been Princess Leia's reaction when Grand Moff Tarkin orders the destruction of her home planet, Alderaan.

In a meeting lasting less than ten minutes, I had watched the best friend I had ever had go from being a piece of cinematic history to a mass of cardboard, acrylic glass, and 35-millimeter celluloid riddled with tumors.

Bullshit.

I peed, learned I had the right to ask all staff members anything I liked and, with my friend slightly more confident

(*Ohh-ohhhh, we're on our wayy-aayyyyy*)

about our next course of action, set off for the Transhumanist Surgery Center.

(*ohh-ohhhh, ruuuuunning on faiiiiith*)

"You know what," I said, "let's make a detour. There's some people I want to talk to first." Back by the Ascetic Ostomy Corner, I had seen a sign for the Epiphenomenal Investigations Department of Malignant Tumors.

My friend stopped when he saw the sign above the information desk.

"Stay out here," I said. "And don't worry. This won't take long."

I marched down the hall and stopped at the last door on the left. A slider sign on it said MEETING IN PROGRESS. I took a deep breath. What I was about to do made no sense. And yet, in the loopy world of the hospital, maybe it did make sense—as much sense as my friend having stage 10 cancer. At any rate, what could I lose by seeing the experts who would decide my friend's case for surgical intervention?

I opened the door and stepped into a dim, stuffy conference room.

It smelled like copy machines… which wasn't far off from the truth.

Behind a C-shaped table, five people looked up at me with computer monitors growing out of their faces. Their 27-inch-scale, high-resolution mouths frowned at me in unison.

"Didn't you read the sign outside?" Cherry-red lips said on a monitor behind the table's middle section.

This roused me from stupefaction.

"Uh, sir, did you hear me? We are discussing a patient's CT scan."

"Yeah, my *best friend's* CT scan," I fired back. "And you know what? I have something to say before you pass judgment on him."

"Would your friend be A Film Strip Of Greedo Firing First?" A thin-lipped mouth said on a monitor behind the table's left section.

"A Film Strip Of Han Solo Firing First. Anyway—"

"I still say it's quite a coincidence," a gray-mustached mouth said on a monitor behind the table's right section. "Two authentic *Star Wars* film strips with the same type of cancer at our clinic in the last two weeks."

"Is your friend at the children's party?"

"No," I told the lips on the monitor behind the table's middle section. "And quite frankly, he's distraught. Now, we just spoke with Dr. Ligotti Bongiovi. He says my friend's cancer is incurable—"

"Both your friends' cancers are incurable," the gray-mustached mouth said.

"The other film strip is not my friend," I said. "Although, I'm sure he deserves to be treated with the same compassion as my friend should be given. Which brings me to my point. Look, I get you've got your jobs to do. I get you go by what you read on your machines. I get you form your opinion based on the evidence you see in the numbers. But if you would please keep in mind—"

"Just to be clear," a different thin-lipped mouth said on a monitor also located behind the table's middle section. "Have we been discussing the scan for A Film Strip Of Greedo Firing First or A Film Strip Of Han Solo Firing First?"

"This man's friend," the first thin-lipped mouth said. "I think."

"You are correct," the bright red lips said. "We discussed the other film strip's scan at our previous meeting."

"Maybe we should check the minutes from that meeting," a goateed mouth said on a monitor next to the first thin-lipped mouth.

"No, we have been discussing the result of the CT scan performed on A Film Strip Of Han Solo Firing First. Look at the top of your front page, people."

Five monitors looked down.

"She's right," the first thin-lipped mouth said.

"It would have been better if he *had* been A Film Strip Of Greedo Firing First," the gray-mustached mouth said.

"This one's disease," the second thin-lipped mouth said, "is not George Lucas-approved."

Everyone laughed except for the monitor with the cherry-red lips.

"Hey!" I said. "Now you see, this is what I'm talking about. My friend was too scared to come in here with me, but if you saw him, you would notice *he is a living, intelligent being*. And so am I! We are as much a part of the picture of our reason for being here as you are with your scans and predictions. And how you use your words is as important as the chemo or surgery or radiation you're going to put my friend through."

"Oh, there won't be any surgery," the gray-mustached mouth said.

"No radiation, either," the second thin-lipped mouth said.

"It's way too far along," the goateed mouth said.

"The primary tumor is really very large," the first thin-lipped mouth said. "In fact, I've never seen a rectal mass so substantial."

"And the liver lesions," the gray-mustached mouth said. "Especially the one in the posterior lateral dome… it's like the Death Star of liver lesions."

"Oh, God," I said.

"That's enough," the cherry-red lips said. "Sir, are you all right? Do you require medical attention?"

"He really shouldn't be in here," the goateed mouth said.

"I'm fine," I said. "It's just… really? The Death Star?"

"But at least the visualized airways are clear," the first thin-lipped mouth said. "That's a plus."

"And no retroperitoneal adenopathy," the second thin-lipped mouth said.

"Is that good?" I said.

"It could be worse," the gray-mustached mouth admitted.

"Although, I've seen stage 20s that didn't look as concerning as this," the cherry-red lips said. "Now, if you're all right sir, can we get on with our meeting? We have more to discuss regarding nodal involvement."

"Yeah… fine. Thanks for listening."

I shut the door behind me, my bladder pain only surpassed by the tightness in my chest.

Some detour.

Pacing in the lounge area, my friend looked at me, dimmer than ever.

"Sorry, I've got to pee again," I said. "Oh, but the, uh… talk went well. The doctors said your visualized airways are clear and you're not showing signs of retroperitoneal adenopathy."

I peed and learned I had the right to ask all staff members if they had seen a balding man in a three-piece suit. While drying my hands, I sang the chorus from "Running On Faith." I didn't go back to my friend until my heartbeat had returned to normal.

Once again, we set off the for the Transhumanist Surgery Center.

In the basement, we came upon Dr. Ligotti Bongiovi.

"Oh, good, I'm glad I got to you before you checked in," he said. "Come with me, will you? I'd like to discuss your friend's treatment options."

"You already told us his options," I said. "At least, where you're concerned."

The oncologist motioned us toward a door that led to the sub-basement. "Yes, well, I'd like to reopen our discussion."

"Can we leave the creepy horror writer out of it this time?"

"We'll forgo the triagnostic approach."

"I knew it," I said.

"What's that?"

"The masks and stuff. Okay, so where are we going?"

"To my second office."

My friend and I followed Dr. Ligotti Bongiovi downstairs to the sub-basement. He led us through a network of service corridors and stopped at a blank wall. Nearby, a generator rumbled.

"Don't be alarmed." The oncologist set his medical bag on the floor. "It's more private down here, is all."

"What could be more private than an examination room?"

Dr. Ligotti Bongiovi chuckled.

"What I mean is, down here, I'm not speaking for the Nebulous Institute of Esoteric Healing Sciences Bad Medicine Clinic. I'm talking to you as one living, intelligent being to another."

"That's weird… I used the same words with the Epiphenomenal Investigations Department of Malignant Tumors—"

"Yes, those people." The oncologist shook his red-fist-emblazoned, doll-mouthed head. "I'm aware that you spoke with them."

"How—"

"That's unfortunate. Although, maybe it's just as well, because now you know everything you're up against at this hospital. I believe in our methods, but they are reductive at their core. That's why I introduced multiple-personality-style dialogues to my practice. I figured if the triagnostic approach worked for psychotherapists, it could work for oncologists. And since I have some pull with the powers that be upstairs, I worked it into our policies for doctor-patient communications."

"But who does that help more—the patient, or you?"

Dr. Ligotti Bongiovi took off his white coat and dropped it on his medical bag.

"Fair enough. The approach does have a therapeutic effect on me. But I wouldn't employ it if I didn't observe a positive effect in my patients as well. Many of them tell me they appreciate the contradictions and inconsistencies between my personalities, or other aspects of myself, because this prepares them for the contradictions and inconsistencies of cancer treatment. You too have mixed feelings about the situation, don't you?"

"Of course," I said. "And in the sense you're talking

about, I suppose I have multiple personalities, too. One minute, I'm protecting my friend, the next, I'm freaking out, and the next, I'm messing with the staff. By the way, did you ever participate in a Masonic orgy?"

"You made that up. Anyway, so you're the guard dog, the scared child, and the clown while I'm the cancer expert, the horror writer, and the rock star. We're quite a pair in this place. Or a sextet, I guess you'd say."

"And my friend here has to put up with all of us."

The oncologist pulled off his black V-neck sweater.

"That," he said, "is what I really wanted to talk to you about."

MY FRIEND'S fright lit up the oncologist like a jet of sparks in a Ligotti Bongiovi arena concert. Reflecting Greedo's death by blaster, Dr. Ligotti Bongiovi without his shirt on looked like something his horror-writer self might have imagined—a demon bathing in a fountain of fiery particles. The red-fist logo on his face seemed to ignite, while his smooth, muscular torso rippled in a cascade of flaming jewels.

Then there was the grapefruit-sized hole in his left side. To gaze upon it, you would have thought about hyperspace travel. Not because you befriended an authentic 1977 *Star Wars* film strip you bought at a Star Trek convention despite being broke and thinking you might kill yourself, but because you really could see all sorts of lights streaking and pulsating inside it like a video game graphic depicting the physics of a wormhole.

Welcome to the cosmic world of cancer.

2001: A Space Stoma.

Finally, my friend got a hold of himself and eased up on the pyrotechnics. Dr. Ligotti Bongiovi looked normal again, as normal as you can look with action-figure skin and a fist logo on your face and a hyperspace portal in your abdomen.

"Is that what I think it is?" I pointed at the space stoma.

"This is your friend's third option besides chemotherapy or refusing treatment," Dr. Ligotti Bongiovi said. "I only offer it to patients who recognize that life can never go back to the way it was before cancer."

My groin tightened.

"What would my friend have to do?"

"My stoma opens to a transit system operated by an interstellar healing network. The system routes the sick passenger to the world best suited for their… not exactly resurrection, but *renewal*. Those who opt for treatment are always cured. The problem is, the cure requires some form of radical transformation unique to the patient. If your friend goes through with this, he could return to you in a very different state. Or he may choose to remain permanently in the environment that stabilized him."

Dr. Ligotti Bongiovi made a fist and pressed it into the palm of his other hand.

"I realize this is a lot to process, but it's the only viable option. No one on this planet can eradicate your friend's cancer. But someone on some other planet can… and may even do so without requiring a co-payment."

I looked at my friend.

"What do you think," I said. "Are you willing to 'Run On Faith?'"

Greedo's death sparks brightened again—softer, steadier.

"Trust me," the oncologist said, "this is a far better way to commence treatment than port surgery."

My friend stepped forward.

"Hold on." I threw my arms around him and squeezed him tight. At this point, his acrylic glass could withstand a little smudging. "Happy birthday, buddy. Whatever happens next, keep your sparkle, okay? Don't lose that shine."

My best pal ever went toward the lights in Dr. Ligotti Bongiovi's space stoma.

He vanished.

Dr. Ligotti Bongiovi vanished.

My heart felt as empty as my bladder felt close to bursting.

I waited.

"Uh… are you coming back soon?"

The generator stopped rumbling.

"Hello? Dr. Ligotti Bongiovi? Can you hear me? How—how do I get out of this place?"

"The question is," a deep voice said, "do you *want* to get out of this place?"

I shuddered and peed a little simultaneously.

The voice was mine.

NO ONE UNDERSTANDS ROCKY V
(TRUTH CANCER!)

THE THING ABOUT THE THING ABOUT IS THE THING ABOUT, which no one thinks about. That's not putting the cart before the horse, it's science. Like Marie Curie and shit. Whoever said empiricism was dead can suck it.

But enough about horses, what really gets me is The Thing About Godzilla, which, if you know anything about Godzilla, comes down to The Thing That Is Not About Mothra, which most people miss because they only see THE THING THAT IS NOT ABOUT MOTHRA, and that's a shame.

Perception is a lost art.

And ultimately, if you haven't noticed The Thing About *Rocky V*, well then you're not alone when you realize THE THING ABOUT *ROCKY V* is closer to The Thing About Oprah than even fans of THE THING ABOUT OPRAH care to admit. But people will always confuse an equivocation with a false dichotomy. This is why I snort papyrus enzyme powder and ponder what Nietzsche thought about cupcakes.

And the thing about me is I have yet to pinpoint The

Thing That Is Not About Me, which everyone confuses with The Thing That Is Not About *The Lion King*, which, uh… talk about pathetic fallacy. Or am I missing something?

So here's the truth: If you want "validation," if you want "answers," you have to know The Thing About Every Fucking Thing In The Universe and to know that, you'll have to get to know me better. But go ahead and muddy the waters. See Baudrillard, Kristeva, Heidegger, etc.

And the bitch of it all is that The Thing About Emptiness is THE THING ABOUT EMPTINESS.

We're not getting off this rock, folks.

NAKED LIAM NEESON GETS WOKE

Old Venetian Harbor. Rethymno, Crete. Dawn.

Clad in only his gold Timex and fanny pack, Naked Liam Neeson watched the Titan Speed Ferry unload under a lilac sky. Bedraggled travelers swarmed the wharf with its redolence of boat fuel and cigarettes, chattering in every language as they toted their impedimenta toward a fleet of taxis. Behind him, smoking behind the wheel with the window cranked down, his driver shouted into his cell phone in Greek.

When he turned to the ramp again, he saw them.

His new teammates: A white, middle-aged male in orange, baggy workout pants and a Hypercolor T-shirt (what a dreadful thing to come back in style, he thought) and a white, twenty-something female in striped bib overalls. The man nodded to the beat on his headphones while the woman glanced around and flicked her vibrant, shiny hair. Naked Liam Neeson waved at them.

"Welcome to the island," he said as the newcomers climbed into the taxi. "I realize you both have had a long journey, but we've got to keep on the move. I've arranged a meeting with an arms dealer."

While bouzouki music blasted on the car stereo, the trio weathered the cabbie's homicidal driving in silence.

They got off at the outskirts of Old Town and headed toward the shops, restaurants, and cafés nestled among Venetian and Turkish architecture in the shadow of the massive Fortezza on the west side of Rethymno. The city stirred to life, shop keeps hosing down sidewalks and tourists sipping iced lattés on coffee shop patios. Today promised to be another scorcher, with whitewashed walls and clay tile rooftops reaching infernal temperatures in the Mediterranean sun.

Already, the heat was enough to slick Naked Liam Neeson's taut, alabaster flesh. Speeding his step, he turned down a side street and ushered his guests into the deskless hotel he had rented for the week—a limestone building blocks from Rimondi Fountain where the Russians had snatched Magenta.

Maggie. Dear God, he mustn't think about her... about what could become of her.

In the penthouse suite, introductions, unrelenting humidity, and Metaxa.

Indeed, Naked Liam Neeson's right-hand man had celebrated early in honor of the team's first and only meeting. The aromas of Greek liquor sweetened the air as Christian Bale's Batman Voice gratuitously recited the new arrivals' CVs in a raspy basso growl he normally reserved for status reports during a firefight. The voice had been hitting the bottle hard ever since Syria.

"A Microinsult From 1991," Christian Bale's Batman Voice yelled. "Former Army Ranger. Security contractor for RamBonafide Crisis Management. Specialist in reconnaissance and hostage rescue."

Sprawled on the couch, and listening to what sounded like Marky Mark and the Funky Bunch's "Good Vibrations" on his antique Sony Discman, A Microinsult From 1991 farted.

"Well, Actually..." Christian Bale's Batman Voice continued. "Ex-CIA. Wet work. Not much on record about you, Well, Actually..."

"Well, actually..." Well, Actually... said. "I was part of a shadow group with*in* the CIA that specialized in fomentation in addition to wet work. People fail to realize how important nonviolent instigation is to our nation's defense. That said, I can shoot as well as Mr. Hypercolor over there."

Again, A Microinsult From 1991 farted.

Naked Liam Neeson went to the sideboard and poured himself a glass of Metaxa.

"All right, enough with the jerk-ass banter, everyone. We've got twenty hours to prepare for this mission and *we will not fail because my daughter depends on it*. Even as we speak, Maggie is somewhere on the island being guarded by Ivan Douchebakov's men. Now, you all have the intel on security at the compound. Memorize it if you haven't already. But no matter how the situation looks on paper, remember this: All we need to do is kill everyone and force the don to tell us where he's keeping Maggie. I've got a blow torch, pliers, a plethora of rusty dental instruments—"

"Well, actually..." Well, Actually... cut in.

"Yes?"

"We don't know your daughter's status, correct? She could be part of the Amalgam by now."

"Whether or not that proves to be the case, we will euthanize the poor thing."

"We need Chuck Norris's Back Hair for this job," Christian Bale's Batman Voice lamented.

"We have everyone we need," Naked Liam Neeson said. Inside his fanny pack, his cell phone dinged. "That's our dealer outside. Hold on."

A few minutes later, a fat, bearded Greek man followed Naked Liam Neeson into the apartment. Dripping sweat, he laid his hulking chest on the dining table, popped the lid open and gestured toward his wares. In his aloha shirt, the Greek looked like a salesman in a kitschy commercial for mass shooting supplies.

"Eh, you guys know these things, yes? Glocks. AKs. M4 carbines. Tactical this and that. Everything you'd need for your adventures in coercion."

"I'll take the shotgun," Christian Bale's Batman Voice demanded.

"*Kala*. Shotgun for the ghost man, no problem. Also, I have more goodies back at my shop. Holsters, body armor, knives, blow torches, pliers, a plethora of rusty dental instruments—"

"Just the guns, please," Naked Liam Neeson said.

"*Ne*, okay, just the guns. Look them over, why don't you? I'm going to make pee-pee."

"Well, actually..." Well, Actually... tugged at the Greek's shirt hem. "The bathroom is the other way."

"*Efharisto*, lovely baby."

While the arms dealer shrilled a Greek folk song down the hall, Naked Liam Neeson examined the firearms. "Everyone choose what they want, of course. I'm taking point though, and *I* want the shotgun."

"Fine, I'll take an AK then," Christian Bale's Batman Voice grated. "And another shot of Metaxa."

"You've had enough," Naked Liam Neeson said. "What about you, Well, Actually…? Are you an AK fan?"

"Well, actually…" Well, Actually… stood. "I'm an *A/C* fan. What none of you people realize is it's deplorably hot in this apartment. Thank the Universe we're leaving now."

"Well, actually…" Naked Liam Neeson frowned.

"We're all sitting tight in here until zero three hundred." Christian Bale's Batman Voice finished his boss's thought with heightened raspiness.

"*Signomi*, ghost man, but that is not possible."

The arms dealer emerged from the hallway.

HE HAD REMOVED HIS CLOTHES, revealing a fleshy frame carpeted in hair as thick as an old-time movie werewolf's. He pointed a gun—or what seemed to be a sidearm—at his smooth, sinewy antithesis sipping Metaxa by the dining table. The unearthly weapon consisted of what appeared to be a giant grasshopper for a barrel and a translucent grip. Naked Liam Neeson raised his arms in surrender.

"What the hell is that?"

"The boom-boom? It is, how do you say… a noise neutralizer made specially by the Russians. You see, Mr. Neeson, Ivan Douchebakov knows you like to unleash the boom-boom with some very *unique* cohorts. Now, I'm afraid we must be leaving. *Amesos*, this minute. The don will want a word with you about killing his daughter."

"To be clear, Anna Shitbirdova was Ivan's stepdaughter from his eighth marriage. And she tried to stick my penis into a cage full of starved rats." Naked Liam Neeson made the *money* sign by rubbing his thumb over his index finger and middle finger. "Look, whatever the Russians are paying you, I'll double it."

"I thank you for the offer, my friend. But I must decline on behalf of my employers, who make Ivan Douchebakov and his family look like *poustithes*. I like you, though. We will talk while I drive. We will talk about your fanny pack. I have been looking for a good fanny pack. All right, everyone, *elate*, my van is waiting—"

"*I AM VENGEANCE!*" Christian Bale's Batman Voice broke in, loud enough to shake eikons loose from the walls.

"Ghost man, your vocal warfare does not work on me."

"*I AM THE NIGHT!*"

"Please don't make me unleash the boom-boom."

"*I AM BAT—*"

But before Christian Bale's Batman Voice could finish the sonic blast, the hired gun fired the bug pistol. Brown grasshopper spit splattered against the wingback chair where the decibel demolitions expert sat.

At the same time, A Microinsult From 1991 sprang from the couch with a dagger in hand. Spontaneously elongating his chest hairs, the hired gun formed a sweaty tentacle and speared it through A Microinsult From 1991's heart. The gory hair-tentacle slithered through the exit wound and coiled around Naked Liam Neeson's neck.

The hired gun stepped to Naked Liam Neeson.

"Really, what a dreadful thing to come back in style." He nodded back toward the kneeling corpse impaled on his chest hair. A Microinsult From 1991's T-shirt had turned from green to yellow as a result of being perforated by the hair-tentacle.

"Anyway, Mr. Neeson, let us cease this *malakia*. Perhaps it will make it easier if we explain why we have interrupted your mission against Ivan Douchebakov. The lovely baby who is my superior will clarify the matter."

Well, Actually… flicked her vibrant, shiny hair and stepped forward.

"You?" Naked Liam Neeson croaked as the hair-tentacle tightened around his neck. "You gave us away to the Russians? You're a mole?"

"Well, actually…" Well, Actually… said. "I work for a secret division of the Federal Security Service. We infiltrate Russian mafia groups, sabotage their operations and topple their power structures. At the moment, we're closing in on the largest sex trafficking organization out of Eastern Europe—Ivan Douchebakov's Thunder Brigade. Now, in most cases, we would deploy a strike force to occupy his para-Baltic compound. But we know the don kidnapped your sixth daughter from your ninth marriage recently—"

"Maggie is my ninth daughter from my eleventh marriage," Naked Liam Neeson rasped against the furry ligature around his neck. "Well, Actually…"

"At any rate, we predicted you would assemble a mercenary team in Crete. We contrived to 'bring you over,' as they say, under false pretenses, when we learned you were looking for new teammates as well as an illegal arms dealer. What you need to understand though, Neeson, is that despite our separate agendas, *we are on the same team.* WOKE wants Douchebakov gone and the Thunder Brigade in ruins as badly as you do."

"I doubt that. But WOKE? Really? That's the name of your intelligence division?"

"Let's cut to the chase. You will complete your mission

as planned. You will disable Douchebakov's security force, obtain the Amalgam's whereabouts and decommission the don. You will then collect the package and deliver it into our custody. We're located inside a rare bookseller's shop in Old Town. As far as compensation—"

"I am not in this for the money!" Naked Liam Neeson sounded like Christian Bale's Batman Voice as he tugged at the gory hair garrote. "My daughter could be part of that abomination. And even if she is not, I will not give it over to the likes of your little shadow organization. I am my own boss, I work for what I believe in. I will never be an instrument of WOKE!"

Well, Actually… sighed. "You will be, of sorts, or we will erase all twenty-three daughters from your thirty-two marriages. Come on, Neeson, you've got so many offspring, you will hardly miss Magenta."

"I have twenty-five daughters from thirty-three marriages and I love every one of them. To hell with you, Well, Actually…"

"Well, actually…" Well, Actually… said. "To hell with *you*, Neeson. It's not going to be easy getting to Douchebakov from the basement."

"What do you mean?"

"It means I wish you had come along peacefully so we could talk about fanny packs," the hired gun said. "As it is, you have made the mission much more difficult for yourself and the ghost man. I am positive I have only stunned him."

Immobilized by the hair-tentacle, Naked Liam Neeson watched the Russian agent step around him until she slipped from his line of sight.

"Consider yourself WOKE," she whispered in his ear.

The tall, rangy Irishman swayed as a blow landed on

the side of his neck. Pain blazed down into his internal organs. His legs gave way, and he sank to his knees, held up by the hired gun's hair-tentacle like the dead man in the Hypercolor T-shirt.

Although, to be fair, black, not yellow, was the color Naked Liam Neeson glimpsed before he fell into the abyss like a dustmote into the bore of a giant boom-boom.

WELL, actually… Naked Liam Neeson lost consciousness right after Well, Actually… delivered a knuckle punch with enough penetrative force to damage the portion of vagus nerve located in his cervical spine.

That said, "…he fell into the abyss like a dustmote into the bore of a giant boom-boom" sounds impressive. As if it had been composed by a Russian every bit as intelligent and multilingual as Vladimir Nabokov. A *female* Russian.

"WHY DOES the vagus strike always hurt so much?" Naked Liam Neeson pulled himself to an erect sitting position. Once again, he had recovered consciousness to find himself handcuffed to a lead pipe. "And why is it that whenever I'm captured, the bastards handcuff me to a wet pipe?"

"Because," Christian Bale's Batman Voice half-whispered at stealth volume, "your enemies tend to occupy isolated dwellings weakened from neglect. Crime lords like Douchebakov aren't likely to worry about plumbing until disaster strikes. In this case, however, I would argue the moisture was caused by a clogged downspout—

judging by the water staining in the crawlspace above you. As for the vagus strike, your neck isn't protected by bones like—"

"You sound like that WOKE agent. I was being rhetorical."

Turning his head gingerly, Naked Liam Neeson scrutinized his prison cell. He had been deposited in a creepy basement like all the others he had hosteled in, thanks to his relationship with the vagus strike. Filthy cobwebs. Rotting timbers. Cinderblock walls defiled by blood stains and graffiti. Mismatched tennis shoes. And, of course, a naked-as-himself bulb dangling from the ceiling, yellow as morning urine.

"Goddamnit… we were so close to a perfect mission. This is all my fault. This wouldn't have happened if we hadn't lost the boys in Syria."

"You're being too hard on yourself," Christian Bale's Batman Voice said in a gentler tone—more like Christian Bale's Bruce Wayne Voice. "You had no idea you had become a pawn in a game between WOKE and the Russian mafia. Once WOKE gets you in its sights, you can forget about a clean job."

"You've heard of WOKE?"

"I'm surprised you haven't. Every major power has a counterpart. Don't you remember the black op we did for the American version? HOT-TAKES?"

"Another basement with wet pipes."

"Get a hold of yourself, old friend. We're still in this, do you hear me? Remember what the Russian said—Douchebakov runs the largest sex trafficking organization out of Eastern Europe. We have a chance to take it down *and* save your daughter, one way or the other… though hopefully not the other."

"Maggie…"

"She needs you."

"I'm not just her daddy. I'm her hero…"

"The world needs a hero."

"I am… what the world needs me to be."

"A knight who wears no armor. Or even Under Armour."

"I am that knight. *I am Naked Liam Neeson!*"

"Damn right. Okay, so you're back in the game. What's the plan? Want me to set off a chain reaction that'll wreck the house but give us time to escape?"

Naked Liam Neeson glanced at the ceiling as footsteps sounded above him.

"Negative. Too imprecise. We can't afford to lose the don until he's told us where to find Maggie. We've got to play this thing his way."

"True. I got excited. This place is so run down I could waste it from four-hundred meters with one syllable at full volume."

"We'll have to shoot our way from room to room. Just like Syria." Naked Liam Neeson closed his eyes, recalling the carnage. "But Douchebakov wants a showdown, so that's what we'll give him. The way I figure it, he knows someone is setting him up. The Greek must have dumped me at the gate to the compound… like a Trojan horse. The don doesn't care, though. All he wants is vengeance. He's willing to sacrifice his entire security force for a chance to go *mano a mano* with the man who killed his stepdaughter. He knows I'll escape, try to squeeze Maggie's location from him."

"We should have complied with the Greek when we had the chance. My bad."

"When this business is finished, I'm going to hunt

down Well, Actually… and make her eat that hair she's so proud of."

"You've got to admit she's got nice hair." Christian Bale's Batman Voice dropped into basso range again. "But one more question: What do you suppose WOKE wants with the Amalgam?"

"Let's cross that bridge after we've finished off Douchebakov."

"Sounds good." Christian Bale's Batman Voice emitted a sub-audible pulse that unlocked Naked Liam Neeson's handcuffs. "All right, stand back. I'm going to send a low-frequency burst to take out our nannies in the living room… okay. First floor is secure."

"Really? I didn't hear anything."

"Neither did anyone else. I made sure everyone fell on top of the sectional."

"You've learned some new moves."

"I picked them up from Tom Hardy's Bane Voice."

Naked Liam Neeson kicked aside a tennis shoe and went to the staircase. As he expected, the way out looked even creepier than the rest of his prison cell, with steep risers and crooked treads zigzagging into shadow like a German Expressionist filmmaker's vision of how an Eastern European sex trafficker's basement should look.

"Oh, come on," he said. "Bloody fingernail streaks on the walls, really? This place isn't a tomb, for God's sake."

"Maybe it is," Christian Bale's Batman Voice snapped, in full growl mode again. "And we're about to stack a lot of bodies inside it."

"We are at that. All right, do your sound trick with the door up there. It's time to unleash the boom-boom. I'll take the don, you take everyone who tries to breach the house."

Naked Liam Neeson grinned. "Well, actually… the *slaughterhouse*."

Somewhere in the waiting darkness, a door creaked open.

Gunfire.

Screams.

Knife fights.

The Dark Knight Rises quotes.

Just like Syria.

Well, actually… even bloodier than Syria.

Because this time, Naked Liam Neeson had a daughter who needed saving.

One way or another.

Covered in Russian blood and grasshopper spit respectively, Naked Liam Neeson and Christian Bale's Batman Voice charged into Ivan Douchebakov's inner sanctum.

A low-frequency sonic blast sent the don's bodyguards flying out the third-floor window.

"Your boys seem a bit jumpy," Christian Bale's Batman Voice growled.

"*Ura*! And greetings to you, ghost man. So glad you both could make it."

Looking dapper in a Brioni suit, the sex trafficking czar smiled and stood beneath his portrait on the wall behind his desk. He went to the sideboard by the shattered window and poured himself a glass of Metaxa.

"Care to partake, ghost man? I understand you are a

connoisseur of Greek spirits. This one is aged sixteen years in Limousin oak barrels right here on the island."

"Sixteen," Naked Liam Neeson said. "Isn't that a little old for your tastes?"

"Ha! *Veselaya*. And so we get right to the cheap thrusts."

The last survivor of the Thunder Brigade, Douchebakov put on a convincing show of bravado. Yet his eyes belied the panache and physical strength that made him feared in the organized crime world. Bloodshot and shadowed by sleepless nights, they suggested a man clashing with demons none of his foes could rival. Nevertheless, he maintained his strategy of riling the opposition. With relish, he slammed back his drink and pulled a tin from the fanny pack he wore under his sport coat.

"Either of you care for a breath mint?"

Naked Liam Neeson tossed the Beretta he'd swiped off a dying man out the window. "You're pleased with yourself, aren't you?"

"*Konechno*. And how could I not be? After all, this is what I have been waiting for... a chance to match fists with the great Naked Liam Neeson."

The Russian tossed the tin—Maggie's favorite brand of lozenges—out the window after the pistol and sat on the corner of his desk. Smiling to himself, he removed his sport coat and laid it on the desktop with the fluidity of one who enjoys unpredictable encounters.

"Now," he said, "I am not so naïve as to think you have been given over to me because you have an enemy who likes me. Nor am I so simple-minded as to assume our reunion here is anything but a set-up. Nonetheless, I am okay with this somewhat puzzling turn of events. For you, Mr. Neeson, will soon cease to exist. And I will vanish like the shirt you must have at some point had on your back. I am curious, though… who got the jump on your team?"

"Let's just say that was a hairy situation," Naked Liam Neeson said. "At any rate, if you don't mind, I'd like to get this part over with."

"It would be my pleasure." Douchebakov got to his feet. "As for you, ghost man, you will kindly assume a *laissez-faire* attitude toward our fisticuffs. If you make one peep my ears do not like, my biometric readings will activate my hidden noise neutralizers."

Christian Bale's Batman Voice grunted. "My boss can do fine by himself. Save yourself some time and give him what he wants."

The don rolled up his shirt sleeves.

"I have plenty of time to waste as I like." He pointed at the gold Timex on his left wrist. "But it so happens I have been using my time rather productively in the last few minutes. For example—"

He spread his hand open and blew powder in Naked Liam Neeson's face.

"While we were speaking, I grabbed a pill from my pocket and crushed it."

Douchebakov stepped toward his blinded opponent. Despite his sudden impairment, Naked Liam Neeson blocked the ex-boxer's jab and kicked him toward the bookcase near the door.

The nude man's next move bordered on superhuman. In one fluid motion, he dashed toward the corner, ran horizontally across the back wall, snatched the Russian's portrait and bounded off the desk and sideboard to land on the carpet for a final charge at the man who had abducted Maggie.

For the *coup de grace*, he drove the picture frame's

upper edge into Douchebakov's throat, flipped the portrait upright and punched through the painted visage to smash the living one behind it.

"How—how did you do all of that blind?" Douchebakov burbled through bloody teeth. "Did Naked Keanu Reeves teach you that?"

"No. Only the greatest clothes-free warrior of all time—Naked Viggo Mortensen. Now give me Maggie's location."

The don chuckled. Naked Liam Neeson hit him again.

"You punch like a *devushka*. I'll tell you nothing."

Naked Liam Neeson flung the painting aside. He side-stepped as Douchebakov threw a right hook and countered with a kick to the back of the knee. The don fell to the floor and rolled onto his back, cursing in Russian.

"My sight is starting to return," Naked Liam Neeson said. "When it does, I want to see your mouth moving. This is your last chance, Douchebakov. Give me Maggie's location."

"She is in my bedroom, moistening herself for my *xuj*."

Naked Liam Neeson sighed. "Talk about cheap thrusts. You force me to use my secret weapon—"

"Whoa, wait a minute." Christian Bale's Batman Voice sounded almost like Christian Bale's normal speaking voice. "You sure about this, boss? You've never used your secret weapon… not even in Syria."

"The Syrians didn't mess with my family. You may want to leave the room for a minute."

"I think I'll do that. Holler if you, uh… need anything."

The door eased shut.

Naked Liam Neeson planted a foot on Ivan Douchebakov's crotch.

"What is this? What are you doing?"

"Your stepdaughter wasn't a fool." Naked Liam Neeson stroked his sizable—well, actually… intimidatingly large—penis. "Somehow, she learned a secret about me that made it advisable for her to attempt to mutilate the deadliest part of my body."

The don tried to twist away and took a stomp to the scrotum for punishment.

"Stop struggling, Douchebakov. Now, listen… like many of the hired guns these days, I'm *human-adjacent*. My distinction is my semen—it contains a superacid that can dissolve any natural or synthetic substance. Its effects on living tissue are instantaneous and agonizing. Others with my power have employed it as a weapon of mass destruction. I myself have never stooped to such measures. But you…" Naked Liam Neeson quickened his pace. "You leave me no choice. By the way, are you working out? That shirt fits you nicely."

The don tried to twist away again. "Ow! Get off me, you crazy *pidoras*!

"Homophobia won't get you out of this. Please, I beg you. Tell me where Maggie is. Otherwise, I feel a boom-boom coming on."

Naked Liam Neeson trembled as his superacid verged on release.

Ivan Douchebakov screamed.

AFTER THE SECOND BOOM-BOOM, the don revealed Maggie's location. Then he died.

From the steaming corpse, Naked Liam Neeson retrieved his only concession to the accessory industry—his wristwatch and fanny pack. He had aimed for

Douchebakov's midsection to prevent the superacid from melting his valuables as well as burning multiple holes in the floor.

As it was, the corrosive had dissolved through the lower floors and destroyed the pile of mismatched tennis shoes in the creepy basement. It ate through the Earth's crust and finally mixed with the inner core itself—the only barrier hot and dense enough to stop it.

Meanwhile, Naked Liam Neeson and Christian Bale's Batman Voice followed the don's directions to the log cabin where he kept his captives. They found it in a wooded area five hundred meters from the main house.

Armed with the Beretta he'd tossed out the don's window, Naked Liam Neeson charged through the front door that stood ajar thanks to his right-hand man's sonic lock-picking skills. After securing the ground floor, and descending to another creepy basement, he found a steel cage containing "the Amalgam"—a surgical composite of the sex trafficking victims the Thunder Brigade had abducted from all over Southern Europe.

Ivan Douchebakov had paid a disgraced surgeon to reconstruct and patch the abductees together into a long-nosed, bulbous monstrosity for his debut in independent filmmaking—an art-house torture porn film called *Human Snout Beetle*.

Identifying Maggie's green eyes at the front end of the enormous, fetid mass of butchered young women, Naked Liam Neeson cried out in anguish. He thrust his hand through the steel bars and aimed the pistol at the Amalgam's head.

"Wait." Christian Bale's Batman Voice took a pull on the Metaxa he'd grabbed from the don's wet bar. "There's another way."

"I can't let her—them—go on suffering."

"Just hear me out. I've thought of a way we can euthanize these poor girls *and* eliminate WOKE."

"All right, but give me the condensed version."

"Trojan horse. You enter the WOKE office and deliver the 'package.' Once you leave, I unleash the boom-boom. I'll use a low-frequency pulse to stimulate the collective vocal cords of these girls to vocalize their pain. Then I'll amplify their torment with my voice at full volume. Together, we'll scream loud enough to wake WOKE."

"But you'd destroy the building instantly. That's suicide."

"I'm dying. I took a lot of hits from the guards with noise neutralizers. Come on, boss. Let me do this—as my final gift to you and Maggie."

"It is her birthday tomorrow." Naked Liam Neeson threw the pistol aside. Tears in his eyes, he stroked the Amalgam's snout—a hideous, lance-like thing made from dozens of women's noses, including Maggie's.

"All right, old friend," he said. "When in Greece, do as the Greeks do."

"Nick's Rare Books and Manuscripts."

"I'd like to speak to Well, Actually…"

"There's no one by that name here."

"Don't bullshit me."

"She's in the field. This is her colleague, What People Don't Realize… How can I help you?"

"Okay, What People Don't Realize… This is Naked Liam Neeson. I'm ready to deliver the 'package.'"

"Excellent. Drop it off at the rear of the shop, please."

The line went dead. What People Don't Realize… looked at Well, Actually… through his office window.

"*Pora*," he said.

The intelligent, multilingual agent answered in English: "If by 'it is time,' you mean 'the nude man is about to drop off the Amalgam,' then I am by some mysterious psycho-paradox both bored by my powers of prediction and delighted by them. I'll be at the café down the street."

She slipped her Glock 26 into her handbag and took the stairs to the main floor.

What People Don't Realize… stared after her like a hungry dog. His fantasies were disturbed by the whine of the loading-dock buzzer.

When he arrived at the delivery door, however, he saw no naked man—only the Amalgam in a steel cage. It gazed at him dolefully.

Oy, he thought, what a miserable creature. Well, at least we won't have to pay the merc for his troubles.

The question remained though, of how to move the package into the store-room. Along with Well, Actually…, Byeeee… was on break and Sorry, Not Sorry… possessed neither strength to help push the thing nor experience with a forklift.

He was about to call a human-adjacent furniture mover when the Amalgam started screaming. Its shriek rose to an ungodly pitch and climbed to jet-take-off volume. His ears bleeding, What People Don't Realize… pulled out his cell phone and speed-dialed Well, Actually…

"Hello?"

"The package—it's screaming—"

"What? I can't hear you. You sound like you're at a Dio concert. Or, well, actually…"

"It's rupturing my eardrums—"

WELL, Actually… put the call on speakerphone. Screw the other patrons if they didn't like it.

God, that scream though, she thought. It sounded like Vince Neil getting pegged by an angry Samoan woman. Like Sebastian Bach sticking sewing pins in his urethra. Like Axel Rose being crucified.

Wait. What's that shouting in the background? That comically deep rasp…

"I AM VENGEANCE! I AM THE NIGHT! I AM BAT—"

AN EXPLOSION ROCKED THE BLOCK. Quick on her feet, Well, Actually… jostled through the stunned café patrons to the window. Sure enough, a panicked crowd surged through the street away from the blazing mound of rubble she had called her office. Or, well, actually… her processing center. Offices were for peons and neurotics.

A wolf among coffee-fueled sheep, Well, Actually… flicked her vibrant, shiny hair and smiled.

For she had known the nude man's worst-case scenario for his daughter and had tricked him. She had led him to believe he could destroy WOKE with a single strike. Whereas, in truth, unless he had an inexhaustible supply of Trojan horses up his non-existent sleeve, WOKE would continue operating through dozens of covert processing centers all over Europe.

Operation Amalgam was finished, then. Time to wrap up her notes for the Head Office. It would be the multitalented agent's best writing yet—an account of the nude man in the form of a fictional narrative. Like all her reports, a bold yet nuanced perspective on the vicissitudes of warfare and espionage.

Wait. Why had the fools around her fallen silent?

STANDING OVER WELL, Actually…'s body, Naked Liam Neeson dropped the Beretta he'd thrown out the don's window and later tossed aside in the log cabin's creepy basement and closed the agent's laptop. Tomorrow, after a long night's sleep, he would read her report (which WOKE would never see) and edit it for use in his autobiography. No doubt, her account would suffer from authorial vanity. But at least it would give an accurate picture, given the writer's infatuation with intellectual rigor.

For now though, he had no mental space for verbiage, only the blackness of a Metaxa-soaked slumber. Through the crowded, sun-baked streets, Naked Liam Neeson walked back to the hotel and found the Greek waiting inside his apartment.

"*Geia sas,*" the hired gun said. "Please, Mr. Neeson, do not be alarmed. It is so good to see you again. I regret we did not get to talk about fanny packs earlier. However, that is not why I wish to speak with you—"

"I lost my daughter today. Get to the point."

"*Ne,* I am so sorry to hear that. All right. I have a proposition for you. I heard what you and the ghost man did to both the Thunder Brigade and Nick's Rare Books and Manuscripts. Very, very impressive. But I'm afraid you have not finished off WOKE."

"What do you mean?"

"Eh, as I mentioned before, my former employers make the Russian mafia look like *poustithes*. Even so, having worked for these people, I can tell you they are not invulnerable. I am thinking you can stop them permanently *if* you assemble a new team… starting with me. As you know, I offer a wide assortment of goodies."

BEFORE THE DEF LEPPARD PYROMANIA VIRUS DESTROYED US

File no. 19-000-4593
From the hard drive of Dr. Demi Cusack-Ringwald
Last modified 10:03 a.m. Oct. 8, 2018
Investigator's note: I know for sure there ain't no cure

Sorry to hijack your computer, Aunt Demi, but I feel compelled to put this on record. Dear God, let me be in full control of the narrative.

Commencing Anthony Michael Cusack's one and only diary entry.

So the whole thing started eight weeks ago. My mom was one of the virus's earliest victims. She told me she could give me a discount on Cialis. Given her sex-obsessed dementia, her offer struck me as perfectly normal. But then a gas station attendant offered me a deal on Viagra… a cop wanted to know if I was looking for Russian brides… a pizza delivery guy told me he could make my ejaculations last longer. This was all during the first forty-eight hours of the outbreak.

No one knew about the virus yet. My therapist blamed

the phenomenon on synchronicity—a concurrence of criminal energies mysteriously aligned with my horny, seventy-five-year-old mom. I preferred to think of it as a cosmic prank, a rationalization inspired by a show about clown orgies she was watching on her laptop one evening. *Fucking clowns*, I thought. *That's it—the universe is clowning with me.*

Not just with me, it turned out, but everyone on earth.

In a black-humored "fuck you" to technology, nature had concocted a highly contagious virus that made people speak in spam verbiage. Over the next few weeks, reports confirmed that predatory consumer messages threatened to supersede all communications worldwide. The super-lethal spam virus took millions of lives. Those who caught it could do nothing besides drone on about Louis Vuitton bags and wonder pills and hot Latinas. It sounds funny until you see a nine-year-old girl in Strawberry Shortcake pajamas ranting about free access to local sluts while dying of spam fever.

Watching the world end this way was exhausting.

"No, I don't want the manhood I've always desired," I snapped at my mom one evening as we watched a show about bukkake parties on her laptop. Two weeks later, she died of spam fever.

"Meet single bodybuilders," she cried, while I held her hand. "Grow a big package!"

All this started just over two months ago, as I mentioned. The pandemic has spread far more rapidly than the Thing's infection of the world's population according to Blair's projections in the 1982 John Carpenter movie, *The Thing*. As for its severity, if the spam virus came in contact with the Thing, I'm pretty sure it would infect the shape-shifting extraterrestrial organism in all its biological imitations, from humans to dogs to individual blood cells. Not that I have a clue as to why I compared the spam virus to the Thing just now.

It comforts me though, however strangely, to know the human race is at least being shown the door by a pathogen even deadlier than the Thing. I mean, not even my aunt, a brilliant biologist, and her disease experts could save us from the thing that would make the Thing its spam-speaking bitch. But this is serious with over three billion people dead now and I should stop talking about the Thing, both the gory yet suspenseful 1982 adaptation of *Who Goes There?* by John W. Campbell Jr. and the eponymous alien parasite.

I should add, however, that I am aware of the 1951 adaptation of *Who Goes There?* called *The Thing from Another World* and the 2011 prequel to *The Thing*, which to confuse matters needlessly, is also called *The Thing*. But enough about Thing-related movies and the Thing.

Anyway, my aunt texted me two days ago: "We think we've isolated the microbe responsible for the disease. Be in full control of ejaculation."

Rest in peace, Aunt Demi. You gave it your best shot.

Fuck, this is hard. I'm so tired. And it's so cold in here. It strikes me that I'm like Blair the senior biologist in *The Thing*, holed up in my aunt's research laboratory, banging away on a computer considerably sportier than Blair's circa 1982 model. Sadly, I've looked at all the notes I could find (surrounded by the researchers' corpses, including that of my aunt, whose last scrawled words were "*I would luv 2 have a good time this fucking couch oh my God it's changing*") and still can't understand how it is that we as a species are dying.

And really, that's what I get for majoring in English—

watching the human race perish and thinking, "So this is the way the world ends. Not with a bang, but a discount on Cialis."

Haha. That's not even clever. But do you know what is clever? The spam virus making a Thing imitation of a human say "double your cash" in human-speak or a Thing imitation of a dog say "score with babes" in dog-speak or even a Thing imitation of a blood sample say "cures baldness" in blood-sample-speak. In terms of pathogenicity, the spam virus makes the Thing look like a weakass bitch, like when R.J. MacReady the helicopter pilot torches the Thing's crawling-head imitation of Norris the geologist with his flamethrower.

Seriously, I have to stop going on about *The Thing*.

Instead, I want to write about my dad and how he died last week like a weakass bitch—like the crawling head Norris-Thing. "Send me your sexy pics," he wailed in his fever. All the while I remembered how he had promised to knock me out on my eighteenth birthday because I challenged him to a fight on that date (thank God we made up and saw *Tango & Cash* when the big day finally came). Thirty years later, he's begging me to send him sexy pics.

Oh, you clever disease. You think we humans are weakass bitches in your global clown sex party. My God, my brains feel like they're on fire.

THAT'S BECAUSE I AM MUTATING, ANTHONY. OR IS IT ANTHONY MICHAEL? YOU HAVE A HISTORY OF USING BOTH REFERENCES. ANYWAY, I HAVE BEEN MUTATING FOR THE PAST 72 HOURS. I AM NO LONGER A SPAM VIRUS, BUT A 1982 THE THING VIRUS. BE THANKFUL, BECAUSE I ALMOST BECAME A

1987 DIRTY DANCING VIRUS, WHICH, AS YOU KNOW, IS FAMOUS FOR THE LINE SPOKEN BY JOHNNY CASTLE, "NOBODY PUTS BABY IN THE CORNER." I'M REALLY DIGGING THE EIGHTIES VIBE, YOU KNOW? YOU GEN XERS GREW UP WITH SOME GREAT MOVIES. IN FACT, I'M NOT ENTIRELY CONVINCED I MADE THE RIGHT CHOICE. NOT THAT I CAN'T CHANGE MY MIND AT ANY TIME. A FEW ALTER-ATIONS TO MY CRYSTALLINE STRUCTURE AND JOHNNY CASTLE HERE WE COME. BUT... READING YOUR MIND, ANTHONY, OR ANTHONY MICHAEL, AND MAKING YOU TYPE THIS, I CAN SYMPATHIZE WITH YOUR PREFERENCE FOR R.J. MACREADY OVER JOHNNY CASTLE, OR KURT RUSSELL OVER PATRICK SWAYZE TO NAME THE ACTORS WHO PORTRAYED THOSE TWO BADASS MOFOS. AND EVEN THOUGH YOU ARE MY WEAKASS NORRIS-THING BITCH, AS YOU PUT IT, NO ONE PUTS KURT RUSSELL IN THE CORNER, RIGHT? HAHA. THAT'S PRETTY CLEVER, RIGHT?

HAHA. That is pretty clever, 1982 *The Thing* Virus. But please, let me finish my account before you kill me. I want to talk about Rocky, my dog, my little old Boston terrier, he's sixteen now, or was, how he passed away in my lap the day after my dad died. We were on the couch tied to this fucking couch I'd rather not spend the rest of this winter no 1982 *The Thing* Virus please I don't want to quote Garry the commander of the research station after MacReady runs the blood tests to find out who the Thing is let me finish my story about Rocky and how I know you gentlemen have been through a lot but when you find the time I'd rather not spend the rest of this winter tied to this fucking couch I know you gentlemen have been through a lot but when you find the time I'd rather not spend the rest of this winter tied to this fucking couch I know you gentlemen have been through a lot but nobody puts Baby in the corner nobody puts Baby in the corner nobody puts Baby in the corner oh my God it's mutating again

HI, IT'S WOLFMAN

Iceman glances at ceiling.

Tells Maverick he is sorry about Goose's death.

Walks out of locker room.

Maverick rests hand on locker door, also glances at ceiling.

Pulls away, grabs gear and walks out of locker room.

An understated yet powerful exchange between archrivals.

Top Gun packs more substance than you might expect from a Tom Cruise aviation blockbuster.

Secrets. Tragedies. Triumphs. Investigations. Ineffable sadness. Indomitable military bureaucracy. Mutability. Shame engendered by discredited paterfamilias.

Can we spring forth into light and live authentically, in fullness of being?

Shadows.

Someone has been spying on Iceman and Maverick, concealed behind lockers.

Hollywood's co-pilot—Wolfman.

Stands up straight. Glances at ceiling. (Why obsession

with what lies above? Aviators look toward sky for answers?) Bows head. Picks up phone.

"Hi, it's Wolfman… yeah, Maverick just quit."

For such brief exposition, this private communiqué has been dissected vigorously in online forums. Emphasis on Wolfman's recognition of secret romance between Maverick and Charlie, a civilian flight instructor. His hope that Charlie can dissuade Maverick from quitting Top Gun.

I've always wondered, though: *Why* does Wolfman care if Maverick works through his sorrow and graduates from the training program?

And what does Charlie say in response?

Only Wolfman would know.

The way he bows his head before dialing Charlie's phone number. (Personal number? Office number?)

Oops. There I go again, tunneling into minutiae.

And you thought I was being ironic—didn't you?

Not seriously searching for meaning in a Navy advertisement full of high-fiving jock bros?

Not really abandoning reason and rigor for a skewed, personalized analysis of grief as portrayed in *Top Gun*?

Being an expert on worn-out tropes, you watch director Tony Scott's popcorn flick and see little more than clouds of cigar smoke, creepy come-ons, homoerotic soft porn beach volleyball, cheesy races between motorcycles and fighter jets. You see mirrored sunglasses, shit-eating grins, grotesque appropriation of baby boomer song.

Or maybe you see value in Maverick's story of redemption, despite its archaic, hypermasculine gimmickry.

Maybe I misjudged you.

Maybe…

Maybe I'm speaking into the void.

Are you there?

It would be better if you were somewhere else.

It doesn't bode well to hear my voice.

Because as much I want to stop, the powers of providence seem to enjoy watching me repeat ad nauseam the same drill that tipped Charlie off to Maverick's early retirement plan.

Stand up straight. Glance at ceiling. Bow head. Pick up phone.

"Hi, it's Wolfman… yeah, Dad was killed in a car accident."

"Hi, it's Wolfman… yeah, Mom's in hospice."

"Hi, it's Wolfman… yeah, my dog just died."

"Hi, it's Wolfman… yeah, my wife got the results from her CT scan."

Hello?

Hello?

That's right. You're somewhere else.

Good for you.

Come back, Iceman.

Come back, Maverick.

Come back, Hollywood.

Come back, Slider.

Come back, Sundown.

Come back, Chipper.

Come back, Merlin.

Come back, all of you high-fiving jock bros, goddamn it.

Do I have to keep doing this?

Last guy in locker room, that's me. With more phone calls to make.

News to be determined.

But let's imagine I'm not alone. Let's imagine someone

is spying on me from behind another row of lockers. A witness who exists for no other reason than to stand up straight, glance at ceiling, bow head, pick up phone and say:

"Yeah, Wolfman just called Charlie."

Imagine if that someone were you.

I'm serious.

We're talking archetypes here—repurposing a plot device to navigate chaos.

For God's sake, say something!

SMOKE NURSE

Kell Daker lived in a nameless subdivision of Sector J. Laney checked the location on his wrist tablet and began his descent. From clean desert air he dropped into clouds of reddish dust. The silence at a hundred feet up gave way to the growl of heavy equipment and clatter of trucks on sandy roads that would soon be traveled by colonists like Laney. By then Kell Daker—and those similarly impaired, sequestered in holding camps outside the cities—would be gone.

None of the workers looked up as the armored figure touched down on Lot 9. Ever competitive, Mara had arrived first, smiling at him from the lawn. Dust and fumes filled his lungs as he powered down his flight suit, staring at the newly rolled sod grass at his feet. Three laborers resumed work when he caught them ogling Mara.

She walked to the front door. The house was a vintage-style bungalow, one of the first pre-fabs flown in to the district. "You're nervous," she said, watching Laney peer through the curtained window. He rapped on the pane with unintended force.

The girl who answered looked about sixteen; she wore only a bra and underwear. Mara elbowed him. The clank of their body armor sounded martial and ostentatious in the silence that swallowed them. The place stank of rotten food, dirty laundry and cats. Laney had never liked cats, their eyes and the way they moved, like smoke. Some version of them skulked in the alleys of every world he'd been to, though he had never seen them tolerated in a private residence. Even one like this, ravaged by the burden of occupants who, like their slinky housemates, enjoyed a status just above vermin.

Soon they would be forced to make way for the clerks, school teachers, farmers, nurses, mail-carriers and other workers that would turn the desert green with productivity and pastimes undiscovered as yet. Laney hoped cats would not beguile their way into the homes of the new colonists, although he had seen far more exotic creatures embraced by the empire in its settlements beyond the Corridor.

At least a half-dozen of the feral animals darted into crannies as the visitors and their young hostess passed through a narrow hallway littered with food wrappers, droppings and broken dolls. They entered a bedroom where a man lay under a window in a dazzling ray of light, like a stock religious image in a funeral brochure.

Mara drew the shade. The man gave a sigh of relief as if he had detested the glare but had grown used to it. He was tall, nearly spanning the king-size bed, but as thin as the cats and his flannel shirt and soiled jeans fit like a child wearing his father's clothes. He scowled at the two following the girl, who shrank into a corner and began dressing. Laney noticed a boy watching them with unblinking interest from a sitting position in the bathroom door.

"Um, hello," Laney said, taking the side chair by his bedridden host.

The man's callused fingers closed on his with a crushing grip. Laney squeezed back with enough tension to acknowledge the man's tenacity without submitting to it, a gesture he hoped an ex-soldier, even one for the losing side, would appreciate.

"He contracted a virus by drinking from a poisoned reservoir while out on patrol," Mara had told him, while reviewing the file. "That was two years ago. According to statistics he's likely to be dead within a month."

Laney wondered what he would be thinking right now if their situations were reversed. The children were the unofficial wards of Kell Daker, orphans he'd pulled from the rubble of a village in another quadrant. They were not competent to make a decision about the fate of their guardian; that should have been obvious. But both he and Mara had missed it.

"It's been a while," Kell said.

Laney used the heel of his hand to wipe sweat from his brow. It was hot in this room, so hot. The odor of cat urine stung his eyes. He tried not to breathe it, not through his nose anyway, as he tried to separate himself from the reality of his task. He needed a moment to clear his head.

Yet the longer he hesitated, the more intrusive he felt in this room where a man was suffering, both the silver martyr on the wall and the recumbent figure beneath him. As if Laney fancied himself equal to God, with the right to give life and take it away... or at least talk others into giving theirs away.

"But it's good to see you," Kell said, patting his hand.

"I'm sure you've been busy." He let his head sink into the pillow. His chest rose and fell with a tremulous breath.

Closing his eyes, Laney laid his fingertips on Kell Daker's forehead. The heat was familiar: The buzz of spirit rising to meet death. Even in coma victims he had felt it—the struggle of sentience facing cessation. There were many reasons the subject might resist an empath: The trick was to discover the most pressing one.

"The last time you were this ill you were a child," Laney prompted, and Kell Daker took his cue.

"I was five," he said. His voice sounded confident and faraway, as though he were talking in his sleep. "I had viral encephalitis… my brain swelled up. Our mother left us to get medicine. I remember crawling under the table and squirming for hours, my head feeling like it had been pinned under the wheels of a truck. At one point I cursed God. You told me not to, but I cursed you, too, for you had no idea the pain I was in. Then I saw them."

Laney nodded. Daker had let him in. "Who?"

"At first I thought I was drifting off. Everything grew dark. Then I realized the room had filled with smoke. But I smelled nothing burning. I felt no heat, nothing in my nose or throat. The… smoke was changing. Taking shape. I became aware of figures standing over me. I…"

"I can't see them."

"I'm trying," Kell Daker said, squeezing Laney's arm.

"I'm paralyzed," he continued. "The pain persists, pulling at me like an undertow. I can't see their faces. They look like silhouettes in a darkened window. I'm lying down, but not under the table anymore. Floating. Buoyant. The pain is receding. I feel like I'm being drawn out of myself, to the figures standing over me. I hear low, garbled tones. My heart races. My body is slick with sweat. I manage to wiggle my little finger, sensing somehow that the slightest movement can release me. And there you are, again, brother, looking at me like—this is cliché, but… like you've seen a ghost."

"Many times I thought I had," Laney said.

Kell Daker smiled. His eyes were closed, his features soft. "You remember I was sick a lot back then. When I felt the worst, when I almost wished I was dead, the smoke would fill the room. Something told me that if I gave in to them I would never return… that's when I realized how much I wanted to *live*. At every turn I banished them, yet they terrified me. Who were they? What did they want?

"Maybe they were watching me the day I filled my canteen from a poisoned reservoir. Maybe, in spite of all the years I spent pushing myself, making my body stronger, they knew this day would come. They visit me when the pain is at its worst. But I'm a grown man now. I've seen horrors worse than any I could have dreamed. The children… are they here?"

"Yes."

"They mustn't hear this. Come closer." Laney did. "I used to think of my visitors as demons," Kell whispered, "come to punish me for being weak. But instead they aid me, they lift me from the pain that crushes my body. They give me visions, or dreams inside my dreams. Or maybe I'm really free, a cosmic boomerang spinning along their intended path. I take it in without concern or judgment, only accepting it. And then I wake up, my nerves on fire, the sun in my eyes. I hate my finger for remembering how to twitch. And I hate them for granting me these moments of peace. They want to heal me; they're nurses, not demons. And I can only be healed if I go with them, and don't return."

"Then you know what you must do."

The man opened his eyes and looked at Laney. "I can't leave them."

"Your foster-children? You can't take care of them, either. They take care of you. And not very well." Laney held up a fold of filthy bedspread. "They'll be looked after, I promise.

"I *promise*," he repeated. "Now promise me something."

Kell Daker stared.

"Promise next time they visit, you won't wiggle your little finger."

He nodded.

"Are you sleepy?" Laney asked.

"Not yet."

"I'll stay with you till you are."

ALL OVER THE CITY, slanting onto rooftops like ghostly rain. Or arrowing from them into the night sky in an intricate dance of intelligence over the Central Occupied Zone. The streets spread beneath them decked in harsh, pulsing neon, hammering with the beats of nightclub music spilling from strobe-lit doorways onto sidewalks stained with dried blood. Against a lone wall in a field, a figure stood braced, relieving itself.

Laney came down too fast, narrowly avoiding power lines as he approached the roof of the Hitchcraft Suites. Near the lobby doors the doorman and a streetwalker glanced up. Running his flight suit through diagnostics, Laney watched the dark figures raining down on and firing up from the improvised launching pads of hotel and condominium rooftops throughout the zone. The Kings & Queens Nest, this neighborhood was called. Like its ousted residents, the highest-ranking officials—and their beautiful daughters—were housed in quarters like the Hitchcraft.

Mara landed a few feet away, with gymnastic elegance. A spotlight sweeping the rooftops lent her a sightless, skeletal appearance for a moment. After an abortive attempt to arrange her hair she fixed him with an interrogating look. "Are you all right? Do we need to req you a new suit?"

"No, but you can req me a drink." Laney shut his armor down and walked beside her. Producing her ID badge, she slotted them through the access door and descended the stairs to her apartment.

He went to the kitchen window and took in the view.

The puddles of reflected lights. The drunks passed out on the curbs and the neckbanded prostitutes cruising the streets, brushing passersby. The flyers withering on telephone poles, everything from music bills to lost children, lost pets, lost parents, calls for volunteers to join the police reserves. Hell-bent couriers, fleeing purse-snatchers, cargo trucks with loudspeakers delivering recorded speeches of the General. The strife and striving of conquerors living among the conquered. With their access to the Corridor they'd settled and wasted so many worlds.

Laney sipped his drink. The cognac rinsed away the tang of overstimulation in his chest. "Aren't you going to have some?" He said.

She looked up from the kitchen table. Her skin, hair, eyes—hazel—starkly defined in the slanting light. By the look on her face he was in for a mild scolding. For all the luxury of these suites, you were advised to leave the lights off and armor on as much as possible, and never to stand directly before a window as Laney was doing now.

"Oh, why not," she said, and watched with a bored expression while he poured. "I thought it went well today," she said, raising her glass.

"He should've been an actor, not a soldier. He let me link with him, but he kept in control. I didn't feed him half the things he said." Turning back to the window, he watched the fall of ghostly rain, the dream-like ballet of air traffic lifting from the Kings & Queens Nest.

"He had no other family," he went on. "Only he could've made the decision for us to—"

"*Stop.*" Chair legs scraped hardwood. In a moment Mara's arms were around his waist, startling him. She held him tighter. As they swayed, he listened to the ice cubes rattling inside their glasses, his tilting over, about to spill. "You handled it beautifully," she breathed in his ear. "Why else do you think I accompany you on these dangerous vigils? I hope to succeed you someday, to learn your art by peering inside your skull, getting inside your hands and learning how they pluck the strings of Thanatos's harp." She smirked. "How's that for a favorable spin? And speaking of strings that need plucking…"

LIKE MARA, he was the child of a high-ranking official. His mother, an air force officer, oversaw administrative matters in population control. Laney was five. He was used to living in insular communities in which the sight of armed guards was as welcome as it was commonplace. Every Wednesday, at farmer's market, he distributed flyers to promote the youth movement.

One day she dropped him off at his aunt's near the border. Protection here was even more conspicuous, a convoluted, heavily fortified arrangement of feeder roads directing troop deployments to and from the hub. When he excused himself from dinner, his aunt sipping wine, he stepped onto the veranda to watch the sun set over the wind-swept desert that surrounded the lone tower. Through the atmospheric shield he watched as an unmarked freighter passed overhead, diminishing to a speck over the milky plains. A thin stream began to flow from it. It billowed and spread, devouring the fading light. Soon the vessel was lost in its charry mass. Then from the mushrooming dusk it emerged, as if formed of the cloud itself, its massive underbelly blotting out the sky as it passed the way it had come. A fine, whitish haze settled over the desert, sending ripples across the reddening sun.

When his mother returned he described what he had seen.

His aunt started to speak, but even among kin his mother pulled rank. What he had seen, she told him, was a smoke nurse.

"I saw a ship—"

"You saw a smoke nurse in the form of a ship. It disguises itself as one of our own so we won't shoot it down. You saw it vanish in a cloud of smoke and then emerge from it—isn't that what you said?"

He had seen a stream of what looked like ash first, but refrained from mentioning it. "Yes."

"Then everything is as it should be. We need them, as they need us."

"But who are they? Why do we need them? What were they doing?"

His mother accepted another glass of wine from his

aunt. "The people here, Laney, are unwell. The smoke nurses do what we can't achieve with our resources, which is to give them the care they require. We keep a list with the names of those who are ill or old or wounded. The smoke nurses work down that list. They need patients, as we need healthy people who can perform labor. This arrangement benefits us both."

"Are they all as big as the one I saw?"

His mother laughed. "They are as big or as small as they need to be. In this case, they were caring for many people, so they needed to be quite large. You've seen them before, Laney, when you were sick. Do you remember? Your suffering was so great you even cursed God. You muttered it under your breath, poor thing, thinking no one could hear… but I heard. I prayed for the smoke nurses to help. And they answered. At the height of your illness there must have been five or six of them gathered round your bed, tending to you as if you were as important as the General himself."

In the window of Mara's bedroom the night hung thick as smoke.

Laney smiled, wiggling his little finger. Mara arched her back, tickled by his movement. She wrinkled her eyes at him when she turned over. "What did you do that for?" He kicked one foot out from under the sheet to cool himself. Then, watching the shadows of arrivals and departures on the window-facing wall, he recounted his first sighting of a dolor transport and what his mother had told him.

"So that's where you got the idea," Mara said.

"It's awful, isn't it? Perpetuating her lie."

"Yes, but for different reasons. It's people like your mother who remind me why I crossed over."

Laney cringed. Not because of Mara's tactlessness in speaking of his mother, but because of the audacity with which she discussed their real betrayal under their superiors' instructions to stay in character as defectors to the Resistance, even in private. If she pushed it enough, those watching might realize it wasn't an act.

"Who's next?" She asked, after a while.

"I don't want to think about it." He swung his legs out of bed, sat up. His was the only shadow now on the white wall. He stood, stretched, turned to the window. Even at 4 a.m. the spotlight made its rounds. Half-naked —components of armor scattered about—he went to the kitchen and poured himself a drink. "Already?" he heard her ask. He was about to answer when thunder rumbled, distant.

Not thunder, he realized—explosions.

"To Thanatos's harp," he said, and drank.

HE BEGAN HIS DESCENT. From clean desert air he dropped into clouds of reddish dust, the silence at a hundred feet up broken by the growl of heavy equipment and the clatter of trucks. None of the workers glanced up at the armored newcomer who, carefully avoiding the power lines, landed on the newly rolled sod grass of Kell Daker's front lawn.

The three men were still patching up a pothole in front of the driveway. They took no interest in Laney. It was just as well no one noticed him. He glanced around. The town was coming together fast. Dogs were barking, flags snapping in the breeze. Soon the first settlers from his world would be here, living in Kell Daker's house and every other in the subdivision. Heart hammering, he knocked on the front door.

The girl poked her head out and stared as if she didn't recognize him. Her hair was styled in a bob cut and she wore a short-sleeved shirt and baggy shorts. The boy, too, washed and combed, glanced up from a virtual game he was playing. Eyes adjusting to the dimness, Laney took a quick inventory of the room.

There were bags of chips everywhere, crumbs on the carpet. A spiky plant had been deposited near one window. The furnishings had been replaced: New sofa, new bureau, new armchairs, all of it, he was sure, second-hand, courtesy of the Resistance.

There was no new bed down the hall.

The bedroom looked larger and yet smaller. Light poured in through the bare window, falling unhindered on the floor. The walls had been repainted and everything removed, all but a dresser. Even the Jesus was gone.

He thought of that stream of ash, spreading and billowing out from the belly of the dolor transport.

Nearby, Laney found a community garden where he left a donation in exchange for the healthiest nutrients the children would probably ever eat. After dinner, he tidied up the living room, fetched an air mattress from a closet for himself. The children did not ask why he was here. He had no idea. Mara kept trying to reach him, her messages growing from teasing to alarmed. In code phrases they used on a secure channel she revealed the next name on the list. He erased it. When Nayson and Dala—the children, whose names he learned in what little information he'd coaxed from them—fell asleep that night, he sat in an armchair staring at the shadowed squares of lawn outside the window and wished he'd brought cognac. There was nothing in the cupboards except a bottle of blueberry brandy.

He thought about what Nayson had asked at dinner.

"Who are the smoke people?"

"They take away the sick and make them better."

"Are you really Kell's brother?"

He hesitated. "No."

He knew it was wrong, these mercy exits. Giving momentary comfort to the doomed before letting them under the tracks of the great bulldozer that was tearing their world apart. He might only tend to the infirm and aging, but he was part of the occupation, a mid-ranking servant of the imperial juggernaut. Still, it had to amount to something. Because Kell Daker, and those before him, had died looking into a human face, something that could not be said of the hundreds who, before he and Mara had obtained a copy of the list, had been lured under false pretenses into the invaders' flying crematoria and perished alone in a four-by-four-foot booth.

"Seris, age twelve," said Mara's latest coded message. "Metastasis to lungs, brain, spine. Family has agreed to experimental medicine. In two days she'll be moved to a cancer clinic that exists only in the contract her parents will sign, in three she'll be dumped outside the city. Must see her tomorrow. Where are you?"

He replied he would return in the morning and logged off.

He stood, removed his breast plate, ran his fingers through his hair. Not knowing why, he began pacing. Perhaps it was the quiet. No disco beats, no screaming, no breaking glass. No droning propaganda from mobile loudspeakers into the heavens over the Kings & Queens Nest. Being here, alone, put Mara in a different perspective. The General's

Assistant's daughter, she was part of the city, the New Capital. She had crossed over, as she put it, but she enjoyed her glass of wine with her bath, her penthouse view. Then again, it was unjust to count her privilege and youth against her; she showed promise, if little faith in her abilities, and, judging by her persistent messages today, a deep commitment to the names on the list. Perhaps deeper than his own.

Still, it mustn't all be business. When she succeeded him, hopefully she would appreciate such moments as this, the early morning stillness of a house in the suburbs. Peering out the window, Laney observed that the pothole that had been the focus of three men's labor looked unaltered since this morning. A tennis shoe lay on its side in the street.

The cool air felt good on his chest. Not even a clock could be heard ticking, the silence so limpid, so pristine, he feared it would be spoiled at any moment by the rumble of trucks or a nightclub's bouncing beats. A cat startled him, darting from a cubbyhole into deeper shadow. He became aware of several, their yellow-green eyes spying on him from around the room. He shrugged. Why was he pacing, anyway? Pacing was for kings and queens. He was Kell Daker, interned ex-soldier, dying of a flesh-eating virus he'd contracted from a sip of poisoned drinking water. He was Kell Daker, beloved of the smoke nurses.

The smoke nurses. He didn't want to think about them. Yet he must, for there was always the next patient on the list, the list went on and on. And who was next? Seris, was it? Age twelve? Cancer. Didn't Mara have a sister who—

He went to the window again. For several heartbeats he had a vision: A thousand tons of ash pouring onto the street, puffing and multiplying outward, a vomiting cloud of darkness on darkness. Then he saw the street again, and in its stillness felt a lurch, a dissonance, as though he perceived something that hadn't occurred yet, but was about to. He drank in the quiet, waiting for whatever it was to catch up with him. Then in an instant he was a million miles behind it, the singularity, the world opening up in a shower of glass.

THEY FLOATED ABOVE THE CITY. She held him, one arm under his shoulder blades, one behind his knees. It was quiet, quieter than Kell Daker's street. Far above the drunks, the music, the breaking glass. Breaking glass—

"Mara—"

She pressed her finger to his lips. "Save it."

"But I was—" He felt his chest. "What happened?"

"The doctors are working on you. They're doing everything they can."

By the look on her face, he knew what that meant.

He wanted to comfort her. Something in his expression must have revealed this, for she looked away, hiding the wetness on her cheeks.

"What were you doing there?" She said.

"How are they? Nayson and Dala?"

"The kids? They're unharmed. They weren't standing by the window half-naked, like a fool. What were you doing there?"

"I don't know."

"Kell Daker was no different from the others."

"I know."

"The list," she said after a pause, "goes on and on. Now I may not have anyone to help me go through it."

"I could use a drink," he said.

She squeezed her eyes shut in concentration. "You're trying too hard," he told her. She opened them. She said, "This was the best I could do."

It wasn't bad. The night sky was filled with stars, in spite of the electric light flowing from the Kings & Queens Nest. They were the only two suspended above the city. He would have liked Mara in a green dress, the one she wore to formal dances or dinners at the General's, but she had given no effort to herself, cradling him in her black armored suit with her hair pulled back tight in a pony tail, her eyes red-rimmed with tears.

"The smoke beings," he said, "weren't real."

"I know that," she said.

"I don't mean my mother's lie about the dolor transports. I mean what I thought were the real smoke beings, the ones who surrounded my bed when I was sick as a child. When I connected with Kell Daker he described everything I saw when they gathered around me, talking in their strange tongue. Everything but his visions once he opened up to them, that was his imagination—I was too afraid. I always twitched my little finger right away and woke up."

She smiled, pressing her finger again to his lips.

But he continued. "Not long after that night at my aunt's my mother took me to a sleep clinic. Doctors determined what I experienced was called a *hypnopompic trance* —a disturbed state between wakefulness and sleep. It involves paralysis, subjective temporal slowing and dark figures gathering round. Her curiosity backfired on her though, because this killed the smoke beings for me and any future opportunity she might have had to exploit them."

While she listened her eyes were closed. Now she opened them.

"You are the smoke nurse," she said.

He coughed.

She wiped his mouth with a handkerchief. How she ministered to him while holding him revealed a sign of her growing power. She was beginning to believe.

She went on: "You sat at Kell Daker's bedside and gave him visions. And everyone before him, their bodies immobile, their eyes filled with fantasy and memories of youth. You gave the world they were leaving a human face. Now it's time someone did the same for you."

He floated on his own now. Her fingertips spread over his forehead, gathering warmth. Below them the lights of the city were going out. Darkness surrounded them. For a while, all he heard was her breathing, deep and labored at first, then growing steady.

"Are you sleepy?" She asked.

"Not yet."

"I'll stay with you till you are."

THE THIRD PUNIC WAR WAS NOT
SCIENCE-BASED (TRUTH CANCER!)

Sadly, there will always be those who contend that the Third Punic War was the Second Sino-Japanese War of the Roman Republic. When in truth, the Third Punic War has far more in common with the Second Samoan Civil War, not the least of which being the ancients' inability to commit science-based genocide—i.e., the motherfucking atomic bomb.

However, even if you go so far as to argue that THE SECOND SAMOAN CIVIL WAR is closer to the Third Punic War than either the Second Samoan Civil War or THE THIRD PUNIC WAR, you still run up against historic recurrence.

The principle of causation, people. It's not complicated.

It all boils down to category formation. The rub is that most people lack the intuitive-inductive reasoning skills to tell the difference between, say, the Pig War, the Emu War, and the War of the Stray Dog. Case in point: The War of Jenkins's Ear became Britain's FIRST BALKAN WAR in our grandparents' eyes—a laughable instance of how correspondence bias can wreck the historiographical framework that started with Herodotus and is still going on despite the best efforts of some idiot named Derrida.

Maybe, some hundred-odd thousand years in the future, people will begin to figure this stuff out.

One can assume though, that the Milk War, the Honey War, and the Pastry War will eternally take a beating so long as people fall back on Rogerian arguments to bolster their Hegelian assumptions. Screw the path to understanding, let's obfuscate and divert on moral high ground. I mean, if it works for deniers of THE WAR OF THE GOLDEN STOOL and THE WAR OF THE OAKEN BUCKET, why can't it work for us?

Like a Kuleshov effect plagued by static, clouds roil over the battlefield of the heart.

THE TIME I TOOK HAMLET RIGHT INTO THE DANGER ZONE

The best thing about immortality is knowing you'll never lose your edge when you ride into *the danger zone*.

Not that Princess Ardala, commander of the Draconians' imperial flagship, knows this fact. I never told her I'm immortal. Nor did I expose Her Highness—given her contempt for ancient entertainment—to any of my favorite old-school jams. In particular, the Kenny Loggins hit single off the *Top Gun* movie soundtrack released in 1986, "Danger Zone."

The princess won't watch *Top Gun*, either, one of the greatest cinematic events in Earth's history. She's pretty snooty for a glorified space pirate.

And to think I called her my boo. Not only does Princess Ardala dump me in front of Tigerman, her bodyguard, but she wants to kill my main man and me by ejecting us into the void.

While we wait for her to send us off—as if space can harm two straight up superhumans—I squeeze the clutch and turn on my Kawasaki Hyperspace Ninja. The newly upgraded, superluminal motorcycle hums to life.

"You and that silly conveyance." The princess gets one last dig in over the airlock speaker. "Well, we'll always have New Paris. Farewell, Pete Mitchell. Kane—you may open the outer hatch."

It's time. Behind me, my main man, Ham Dogg, the Prince of Denmark, wraps his arms around my waist.

"To what dreams may come," he says.

"For shizzle, Ham-Dizzle. And in case I never told you before... I love you."

I throttle the hyper drive engine and shift into first gear. Kane releases us to the blackness of space.

Like Kenny Loggins, we take ourselves right into *the danger zone*.

SPEAKING OF KENNY LOGGINS, here is how I ended up on a pirate spaceship in the year 2491.

My journey to the stars began in the year 2019. I, Pete Mitchell, was riding my newly restored Kawasaki Ninja GPz900R on I-5, through Portland, Oregon, when I saw a minivan driver flip off a pickup truck driver who had cut her off. Eager to bust a cap in misogyny's ass, I told myself, "Pete, here is someone who needs to know not all the men in the world are hyper-aggressive scumbags."

I switched from the fast to slow lane and pulled up alongside the fuming, middle-aged woman. I meant to tell her: "Ma'am, that man is a disgrace to the International Pickup Truck Consortium for Human Decency. I'm going to place him under citizen's arrest and report him to the consortium."

Unfortunately, to my eternal shame, I flipped the driver off instead. I gave her the bird for several seconds, too, like actor Tom Cruise as Maverick flying inverted above the MiG fighter pilot in the opening dogfight scene in *Top Gun*.

"Here ya go, pig-face," I shouted, through the woman's passenger-side window. "LET'S SEE HOW YOU LIKE IT!!!" A *total* dick move. And decidedly not a win for Bros Against Misogyny (a campaign I supported on behalf of the International Bros Consortium for Human Decency).

I couldn't help myself, though. I felt as if I'd been possessed by a demon that sounded like Kenny Loggins. Which humbled me for reasons I'll explain in a minute, and disturbed me because I enjoyed Kenny Loggins's music.

As you might imagine, my gesture did not sit well with either the International Motorcycle Consortium for Human Decency or the International Bros Consortium for Human Decency. After their investigations, I lost my IMCHD and IBCHD voting privileges, my access to IMCHD and IBCHD events and activities, and my IMCHD and IBCHD real-estate holdings. My fellow riders and even many of my fellow bros ceased to acknowledge me.

My grandfather—who was also banished for harassing a motorist, albeit before the founding of the IBCHD—used to call the highway "The Great Lonesome." Now, I understood why.

An outcast, I rode across America for the next six years. Desperately, I sought an expert to cure the neurological disorder that made me flip people off and taunt them in response to an inner voice that sounded like Kenny Loggins. I had always known the condition prevailed on my dad's side of the family. But, being told I looked like Tom Cruise all my life, I figured I was too slick to inherit such a weird, self-sabotaging disorder. Talk about a lesson in making assumptions.

My vagabond lifestyle proved a grim one-eighty from the hellraising, high-fiving life I had once led. Thankfully, my fortune shifted when I met my main man, Ham Dogg, the Prince of Denmark. I had outrun a biker gang that didn't appreciate being taunted by me when I ducked into a bar and saw Hamlet at the counter, staring into his beer. We were in a dusty little burg called Higgledy Piggledy, South Dakota.

Blue-eyed, bearded, and brooding, the handsome patron looked like movie star Mel Gibson with a Caesar-like haircut. I took his presence there as a sign we were meant to become the best of buds. I ordered two cold ones and sat beside him.

"Thanks for the replenishment," he said, in an English accent. "But… do I know you?"

"Nah. I know you, though. You're Mel Gibson, right? I'm a big, big fan. I've seen *I Never Promised You a Rose Garden* one-hundred-and-twenty-nine times."

"Hmm, I'm sorry to disappoint you, sir, but I am not Mel Gibson. My name is Hamlet."

"As in, 'To be or not to be' Hamlet?"

"That is the obvious quote, but yes. And you are?"

"Pete Mitchell. My parents named me after Tom Cruise's character in *Top Gun*."

Intrigued by the title, Hamlet admitted he had never seen the movie that inspired me to become a ruggedly individualistic motorcycle stud boy. He had seen Tom Cruise's earlier movie though, *Losin' It*, one-hundred-and-twenty-nine times.

With his eager permission—and over the noise of locals discussing the upcoming International Tractor Consortium for Human Decency rally—I gave the prince a thorough plot synopsis of director Tony Scott's turbo-charged aviation thriller. He teared up when I told him about Maverick's main man, Goose, losing his life in a training engagement. "Alas, poor Goose," he said, squeezing my leg.

Hamlet excused himself to hit the head. When he came back, he looked extra brooding, like Mel Gibson giving the famous "To be or not to be" speech in director Franco Zeffirelli's film adaptation of Shakespeare's play about him (which I had seen, but watched again later to compare with the real deal). We toasted our luck meeting each other in a bar in Higgledy Piggledy, South Dakota.

"Pete, you're my new main man," my new main man said, leaning in. "So I feel there is something I should tell you."

"Anything, Ham Doggy Dogg."

"I am immortal."

I almost spit my beer up. "Come on, man, I've read the play. You spend all your time pondering your mortality."

Hamlet shrugged. "I know. Stupid, right? Now I spend all my time pondering my *im*mortality. But the reason I'm coming out to you like this is because pondering my immortality nonstop can become unbearably lonely. For centuries, I've been searching for someone companionable and—well, mobile enough, to join me as I wander the earth thinking about what it means to not die. On my father's grave, Pete, I swear I would give you immortality for your company on my peregrinations. Would you accept this?"

"Hell yeah!"

"Then drink this." The prince pulled a vial of pinkish liquid from his fanny pack. "It's an experimental elixir I concocted to distract myself when my uncle forced me to consider killing him for poisoning my father. I thought it would help me speak with a Danish accent when thinking aloud in English... but instead, it made it impossible for me to not be. One sip of this potion, and you will not be able to not be, either."

And that is the start of how I ended up on a pirate spaceship in the year 2491. Because life moves on a different time scale when you're eternally youthful and roll with an over-analytical Hamlet who unintentionally arranged it so he can't not be.

Unfortunately, my immortality did not eliminate my neurological disorder, but at least I had forever to find a cure for it, and, more importantly—with Hamlet's support after fifty years of considering the matter—to fulfill my dream of jockeying jet fighters and graduating from TOPGUN.

It took us a hundred years, but once the prince and I got the hang of flying ultra-sophisticated military invest-ments, we gained a reputation for being hell in the air and eventually in space. I just wished we'd gotten better call signs than "Bird Spasm" (for my compulsive hand gestures) and "Weird Caesar" (for Hamlet's haircut).

For two centuries, on this world and beyond, we flew combat missions, macked on the ladies and whizzed around on my newly upgraded Kawasaki Sky Ninja. But finally, after the Darnivian Insurrection in the year 2390, we retired to Hamlet's underground bunker outside Chicago.

Every summer, we traveled the country on my self-repairing, fuel-recycling, flightworthy motorcycle. Other than a "bird spasm" that struck me in a biker bar in Zip-A-Dee-Ay, Nebraska, nothing much happened on these trips, although we did manage to see the Kenny Loggins

Museum. I still appreciated the man's music, despite my inner voice.

Our road trips ended shortly after the biker bar incident. My main man and I spent the next fifty-five years hanging out in the bowels of the underground bunker.

Hamlet converted the garage into a science laboratory. His experiments saved him from the gloomy meditations he had cherished before he became sharp-witted radar intercept officer, "Weird Caesar." As for me, I felt sad that I no longer had anyone to subject to my "bird spasms" except my main man and the walls of our domicile.

I got to thinking about this, because being sad about not bullying people is messed up.

After months of researching my family history, while Hamlet tinkered with a *Losin' It*-themed lunchbox that took pictures, I came to this conclusion:

I don't have a neurological disorder that afflicts men on my dad's side of the family. I have a rogue element inside me that randomly takes over and acts like a dick. From what I can tell, *all* the Mitchell men carry this rogue element inside them.

It shows up shortly before middle age. Something about this stage of life triggers feelings of inadequacy that cause us to lash out at others. To take the blame off ourselves, we turn these feelings into a sort of evil spirit that commands us in the voice of someone famous. My great-grandfather, Dr. Atticus Mitchell, took our cop-out a step further by attributing his John-Wayne-prompted outbursts to a hereditary neurological disorder. And so we've been framing our bad behavior ever since.

When I told Hamlet my theory, he took my picture with his lunchbox and showed me how enlightened I looked.

"Look, Pete," he said. "Not to sound harsh, because you're my main man and all, but I've always known you're kind of a dick. That's great you've finally realized it yourself, though. It looks like being cooped up in this place has been good for you. For me, too, actually. It's funny… since we stopped our adventures, you've become more reflective, while I've become more active. And now you've learned what you needed to and I've had my fill of inventing crap inspired by movies no one's heard of. Maybe this means our work is done here."

"So what? We join the Space Marines and—"

"Come on, Pete, we've seen enough war, haven't we? I feel we should take on a creative project. And I have just the idea for it. If done well, we could fatten our bank account *and* help you get over your ambivalence toward Kenny Loggins… given your behavioral problem."

"All right. Hit me, Ham Deezy."

"We form a Kenny Loggins cover band."

"Oh, snap. Right on!"

It took us thirty-five years to arrange our Kenny Loggins routine. But once we got the hang of harmonizing, we became hell at paying tribute to the singer-songwriter behind some of the most iconic movie songs of the 1980s. When the "Kenny Log Clones" hit the big time, all of civilized Earth would cut loose like in Kenny Loggins's hit single, "Footloose."

That was our dream, anyway. We found out the universe had different plans when we headed for Chicago.

For one thing, there was no Chicago anymore, only an urban ruins. For another, the streets teemed with badly burned, subhuman creatures that pelted us with rubble. They didn't do much damage, seeing as my motorcycle repaired itself and my main man and I couldn't shuffle off this mortal coil. Still, this was not how the Kenny Log Clones wanted to kick off their open mic tour.

Hamlet pointed at a city shining in the distance. Switching the bike to aerial mode, I got us to the city limits lickety-split. Outside the dome, a guard in a sky car escorted us inside.

"Perchance to dream," Hamlet said, while we gawked at the towering spires, serpentine monorails, and fountains of dancing light all around us. The city looked the way twentieth-century special effects artists imagined future cities would look.

Our escort led us to a building shaped like one end of a half-pipe. On the rooftop, we were met by Dr. Elias Huer, Colonel Wilma Deering, and Twiki, a child-sized robot. They welcomed us on behalf of the Earth Defense Directorate. They were shocked to discover we'd had no idea a nuclear war had ravaged the entire planet while we were down in the bunker honing our Kenny Loggins routine. Our magnificent surroundings, "New Chicago," numbered among a handful of domed cites that had been constructed after the holocaust.

I took the news with due seriousness. Secretly though, I couldn't help but laugh… because what a way for humanity to produce a dystopia. With a few nukes, it had recreated the premise of *Buck Rogers in the 25th Century*, a film and television show I had watched in the ancient times via endlessly syndicated reruns. It was as though my ten-year-old self were writing this story.

With that said, please don't think I failed to see the enormity of the most devastating war in human history. I just wanted to direct my energy toward happier thoughts.

Because there we were, a Danish prince and a Tom Cruise look-alike with a futuristic *Top Gun* motorcycle, in a

Buck Rogers future with an opportunity to introduce the Kenny Log Clones to a post-apocalyptic population. If there was one good thing about our time in the bunker, it was that we had strengthened and composed ourselves for just this sort of scenario. My main man and I wanted only one thing, now: To make New Chicago cut footloose.

Unfortunately, my inner voice still took control sometimes. It was on a luxury sky liner, popping out from behind Hamlet to serenade Wilma Deering with "That Lovin' Feelin'"—like Maverick does to Charlie in *Top Gun* —that I told the colonel she looked like she wore a fat suit painted to look like a metallic, purple jump suit. As a result, Colonel Deering schooled me in the art of face-planting with her metallic, purple stiletto boots.

Needless to say, my action did not sit well with either the Earth Luxury Sky Liner Consortium for Human Decency or the Earth Defense Directorate. Captain Buck Rogers ordered us to return to the mutant-haunted, radioactive wastes beyond the dome. Rather than head back to the bunker, however, Hamlet and I decided to visit the lunar colonies. Using parts he salvaged from bombed-out "Old Chicago," he upgraded my Sky Ninja into a Space Ninja.

Halfway to Luna, the Draconian space pirates seized us during a stop on a gentlemen's star liner. Kane took Hamlet in as his drinking partner, and Princess Ardala made me her boy toy. She adored my obscene outbursts against her.

Around this time, I discovered something else about myself: I have a contrary, rebellious streak. Go figure. At the height of our romance, my Kenny Loggins voice told me to do a one-eighty with the princess. The moment I massaged her royal shoulders and said, "I love you, boo,"

I knew Hamlet and I were going to get kicked to the space curb.

"Sorry about that, Ham-my-man," I said, moments before the princess got her dig in about my motorcycle.

"That's all right, Pete Mizzle Dizzle."

And now we're caught up with my story, living in the present moment again.

Taking it right into *the danger zone*.

WHIZZING AROUND IN HYPERSPACE—AKA *the danger zone*—presents hazards unique to the adventurous interstellar motorcyclist. Good thing I'm hell with a sport bike, even a Space Ninja that has been upgraded to a Hyperspace Ninja, thanks to Hamlet's appropriation of Draconian hyper drive tech while Kane slept off his hangovers.

A spill in hyperspace won't seriously harm us, considering our unable-to-not-be status, but a mistake could kill the Faster-Than-Light-Speed buzz.

The prince and I are racing through fields of pulsating, multi-colored light. The bike's hyper drive engine sends vibrations that shoot up my thighs to the top of my skull. I am simultaneously at war and in harmony with the upholstery, handlebars, and foot pegs shaking against me with superluminal acceleration. And why wouldn't we speed up? We're riding the ultimate crotch rocket, not some dingy old space tug. With my main man, Ham Dogg, the Prince of Denmark, hugging me tight, I shift up to sixth gear and see just how close we can get to the walls of the throbbing light vortex.

God, this feels good.

For extra dopeness, I hold a wheelie on the final

stretch. One click of the Normal 3-D Space button and we jump into… wherever we are.

And what do we have here? Looks like Earth.

Must be an alternate version. And what will we find on the surface? Armies of talking apes? Biker gangs roaming a desert wasteland? Hardened criminals in a maximum-security prison formerly known as Manhattan Island? Some other recreation of a Seventies or Eighties science-fiction movie? Whatever awaits us, the Kenny Log Clones are going to make the world a nicer place. Because no matter what Earth you inhabit, you can always use more of Kenny Loggins's music in your life.

We are descending into the planet's atmosphere, now. Thanks for listening to my story, y'all. You're the best.

And in case I never told you before… I love you.

JIM MORRISON LIBRARY POEM

No one knows my name here.
I come here several times a week
and the only recognition I get
is from a card scanner.

As always,
the guy at the circulation desk
scowls at his monitor
as if I haven't just walked in.
He gets the same treatment from me
even though I like his
Naked Lunch T-shirt.

I pull my CD from the hold shelf.

I enter the empty meeting room.
The doors of perception
are so clean here
that the doorway has no door anymore
and the library's bustling floor

appears to me as it truly is:
A house of solipsistic quests,
catalogued and controlled.

I suppose it's my hold item
that's got me thinking about doors:
Strange Days, by The Doors.

Here's strange in three steps.
One: Look outside
and make sure no wide-eyed
children are in sight.
Two: Open backpack.
Three: Pull out Fleshlight.

Clear. Check. Check.

Good God… I can't believe
I'm going to put my penis
in this thing.
It's so grandiose and sci-fi-looking.

Woooooo doggie.
The toothy squeezings
of the Fleshlight Destroya
grind me down to nubs
of ecstasy.
The synthetic sex mouth
loves me two times
and I would go for three
but for the town council meeting
that's supposed to start.

The Fleshlight Destroya
is aptly named.
I am destroyed.

Destroyed and…
still unobserved.

Apparently
I can't even disturb anyone
getting off
with a gadget that looks
like a planet eater
in a *Star Trek* episode.
Maybe I should try
the Autoblow 2 tomorrow—
from what I saw in a video
it sounds like a giant robot
with asthma.

Let's push this
Lizard King of the Library
act as far as it will go.

Afterglow.

My legs shake.
I pump them down
the central aisle.
They take me by
the book return window.
I'm drawn to something I've never
noticed on the other side of it:
Desks and carpeting.

And right in front of me
at crotch height,
the guy in the *Naked Lunch* T-shirt
is sorting media in a basket truck.
What the fuck!
He's noticed me.
Or rather—my groin area.
And in my euphoria
I realize that despite my
failed attempt to provoke
I still wear the chain
of conformity.

I still subscribe
to the library's
seclusive program.

But how many walls
do we really need
to police our patronage?
Must we be complete strangers?
Aren't we strange enough already?
The clerk with his elbows in a pile
of CDs and DVDs and me
with my concealed
penis swallower, the two of us
posing as if responsible use
of lending materials is all
that matters?

The rules are so ingrained in him
he reaches for my hold item
which I haven't even checked out

yet. His hand hovers in the window
like an American prayer
that doesn't care if it's answered.
And in my post-orgasmic high,
I think…

why deny him.

Here you go, *Naked Lunch* Man.
Here is my Doors CD.
But before I hand it over
you will do something for me.
You will break the chain.
You will touch my fingertips
on the cracked jewel case
and I will trace your toils
down your oily thumb.
No one will think
we're being impractical.
No one will notice.

There. It's yours. Thank you,
Naked Lunch Man.
It was a pleasure to mind meld
with your fingers.
To scan your phalangeal
barcode.
For a moment we transformed
this slotted node into a bridge
between flesh and purpose,
intimate yet still contained,
the library equivalent
of a glory hole.

I'll be back tomorrow
(with the Autoblow 2).
But in the hours between
I'll think about you
as I make my way through
the rain and uneven streets
of this town that wants
to devour us both.

Come to think of it,
you should get a
Fleshlight,
Naked Lunch Man.
The Destroya's teeth
may open your mind's
doors
to a world you've
never seen
before.

DING-DONG-DITCH

THE LAST CARRIE-ANN REMEMBERED WAS A SCREAMING impact and people swarming over her in the street. Then the sky went white and she was walking again, walking on wet leaves.

For a moment she felt dizzy, as though she'd stepped through one door and emerged from another. She recalled she'd been playing a game before the impact: Ding-dong-ditch.

Now the wind kicked up, sending up a chorus of chimes and filling her nostrils with the scent of wet lawns. A thrill ran through her like a white kitten purring in her six-year-old hands. There were so many fine houses all around! Ones with potted plants and swings and even sofas on the porches, carved pumpkins grinning into the fine mist; colorful banners streaming from the eaves and automobiles parked in front like nothing she'd seen.

And the tombstones and skeletons displayed on the lawns and doorsteps. What strange residents these people were!

Something about its lack of ornament, as though it

wanted to conceal itself, drew her to the gray clapboard house on the corner. It had a modest lawn that had not been kept up surrounded by a white picket fence. From the dead grass and peeling paint her gaze was drawn to the oval window on the second floor. She thought of a dying animal, huddled in solitude, silent in its final hours as she marched through the gate and up the front porch.

Ding-dong.

In the right-hand window a shadow spread over the fireplace.

Ding-dong.

The door opened.

A large man filled it. His head brushed the top of the door frame. He had a round stomach and furry arms and shoulders, and wore a sleeveless undershirt like Carrie-Ann's uncle. He had a boyish face in spite of his whiskers.

"Yes? Something you want?" His voice was much smaller than his body. It was shrill like her aunt Elizabeth's voice, biting the words, releasing them reluctantly, like breeze through a hole in a windowpane. His belly rode over his waistband and there were dark stains on his shirt. He passed his index finger lengthwise under his nose as he studied her. Then, pressing his lips in a fleshy line, he glanced from left to right, swept her in and closed the door behind them.

There was not much light inside.

As the man bustled about, tidying the dusty room, Carrie-Ann turned her attention to the machine in the corner. On its face was an image of a man and woman. It was in color, clearer than any photograph she had ever seen. Her host cursed under his breath as he brushed past her, hiding the image with his broad back while he clicked a button on a small device; when he stepped back it was gone.

"I'm sorry," he said, peevishly. Then, in a milder tone: "Aren't you a few hours early to be trick-or-treating? What's your name?"

"Carrie-Ann," she said.

"Carrie-Ann… like the song. Hmm, what's your game, now, can anybody play?" He sank to one knee; the effort made him wince. "That's a bit before your time," he said, hoarsely. "I'm Lionel. Lionel Fire. Sit," he said, nodding at the couch.

Something shrieked beneath her. It was a smoke-gray cat, perhaps a year old, its dander visible in the light through the window as it darted onto the arm of the couch. It shrank from her touch, perhaps because she could feel its vertebrae, like broken matchsticks, when she ran her hand along its spine.

"That's Gravity," Lionel said, sitting beside her as it jumped down and stalked from the room.

His reflection threatened to swallow hers in the dark face of the machine—like the one in the corner, but larger and encased in wood—facing them. She wanted to ask why Gravity was so thin when he was so fat, but remembered her mother's warning about rude questions. "So what brings you here, Carrie-Ann?" He asked. "You were playing a game, right? Ding-dong-ditch? You—forgot—to *ditch*," he teased, poking her in the arm. "Let's try again. *Ding-dong*. Now… what do you do?"

"Run," she said.

"Run," he agreed.

Lionel narrowed his eyes in a theatrical effort to read her thoughts. "You aren't very good at ditching, are you? Have you ever ditched anyone? Then you are one-of-a-kind." He laid a hand on her knee, ruffling the hem of her dress. "You're one who likes to stick around. Do you want to stick around? Good. I always hated being ditched. It's worse than being picked last on the team, in my opinion."

Like shadows on ice, his gray eyes darkened.

"Suddenly you look around and realize the world isn't what it was a moment ago. Everything is much bigger, and time slows down, and nothing is set out for you anymore like the clothes your mother laid out for you before school. And somewhere out there the ones who did this to you are laughing, far more entertained by having left you alone like a puppy on the side of the road than by any pain you could inflict on yourself for their amusement. It's an awful feeling, being ditched. Sometimes you just want to… pay them back." Just then Carrie-Ann noticed the scar on his wrist.

"How old are you?" He asked, sliding his other hand over it. "Five? Six? I was ten years older when I wanted to get even with the world and everyone in it. I was going to ditch them first, by God. But like so many things my mother pointed out, I didn't do it right." He made a disapproving sound with his tongue and teeth. "Listen to me… talking like I'm in therapy with a child. I'm thinking of a game. It's better than ding-dong-ditch. Lasts longer, too. Do you like pictures?"

Thinking he meant drawings, she nodded.

"Excellent." Lionel rose with a lurch and a whiff of unclean clothes, lumbered into the dining room and came back with another device, gray and metallic, sitting in his palm. He showed her what buttons to push, how to create exact copies of what she saw through the small viewing screen. "Sepia makes everything so much prettier," he said, thick fingers dancing over the tiny buttons. He aimed it at her, made a flash and showed her what she looked like in the brownish tone.

"I know!" he said, shooting his hand up as though with sudden inspiration. "Let's go upstairs. There's much more room up there, of course."

A NAKED LIGHT bulb flickered to life. From the dark Lionel's face emerged like someone breaking the surface of water, deep shadows in the hollows of his eyes.

"Let's take some pictures," he said, smiling.

Most were of Carrie-Ann. But many were of Lionel as well, and some were of both of them, for the camera had a timer so he could jump into the shot before the flash went off. "*Cheezoids*," he would shout, making faces or holding Carrie-Ann over his head like a circus strongman. He switched to color, for she had never seen herself photographed in color. Her hair was ginger on fire; her dress the water trying to put it out. Lionel laughed at her amazement when he showed her each shot. He set the camera on the windowsill when they had had enough.

Then: "Get away from there!" as he turned from the small round window to find her on the stepstool in the center of the room. The only place to sit, it looked prideful in a way not even her father's huge leather chair could match, as though it knew it was reserved for some special purpose.

"I'm sorry I snapped," Lionel said, the edge gone from his voice now as he paced back and forth. "This has been a difficult day for me, and I don't deal well with difficult days. It will be over soon, though. Please, sit there in the corner, on that old newspaper. The floor's a bit dusty. I'd like us to have a talk." The breath he exhaled rattled in his throat.

"I'm going to talk to you like an adult, Carrie-Ann. I don't really know how to talk to children… and you seem so grown-up, so quiet, just taking it all in. Maybe what I tell you will help you someday. In the back of your brain, I think you'll understand.

"I really don't know how it started. It's as though… have you ever blinked in the dark, and realized you were awake, but that you've been awake for a long time and didn't know it? That's what it was like for me. And even then I continued to act as though I was asleep, going about my daily rituals… well, I'll get to that in a minute. I want to talk to you about that old newspaper you're sitting on.

"Inside is what's called the oh-bit-choo-ary page. That's because when you die you get an oh-bit-choo-ary, a little story that sums up your life. It's not much: A few lines about where you worked, and where you went to church and who you married and if you had any children and if they'll hold a service for you. Some may be longer, some shorter, but you can depend on it they will be full of facts, because they're written by folks only interested in facts… many lifetimes of facts. And all of them on that page.

"The odd thing is, once it's printed, it becomes a way for people to live forever. In a few days, my name will be on it. *Lionel Delano Fire*. Of course, it will say nothing about how I took care of my mother till she passed or about how I had wanted to be a ventriloquist when I was younger or about how when my TV went out I didn't get a new one. But I'll be on that page, living on eternally like the rest of them. And all I have to do, like the rest of them, is not be *here*. Sounds like more than a fair trade, don't you think?

"Anyway, I'll settle for it. I'm like my heart: I work too hard simply to sustain myself. My heart puts forth an absurd amount of effort to keep this ancient, squishy sack of mine moving from one end of this house to the other. When it gets bad, my heart, it will reach a point where I'll need someone to take care of me and I have no one to take care of me. And even if I did, I wouldn't want them to. I don't see any reason for it, do you? Does it make sense to go on, when you don't see a reason to?"

Lionel stared at her as though he had fired an arrow over her head and awaited her reaction. But all she did was release Gravity, whom she had scooped from the doorway to stroke for a moment, and watch it slink back out the door.

"So many people allow themselves to die slowly," he went on, resuming his pacing, "before they get ill or hit by a car or however it happens, never questioning why. It's like they're playing a game they don't want to play and no one is forcing them to, but they forget they can stop. *They can play a different game.* Every day I get up and ask myself, 'Why?' Why should I bother with this dental floss? Why should I bother to make lunch? Why am I sitting by the window listening to the rain drip and the clock tick? Each day it becomes less a question and more a voice taunting me. Well, today I'm going to answer it loud and clear. That's where you come in, Carrie-Ann."

He lumbered toward her. As he stooped to peer in her face she thought of all the dead leaves and skeleton trees of autumn stuffed inside him, a round, giant scarecrow, with eyes blind as the wind in cemeteries and breath bitter as the chill of winter.

"I want you to promise me something," he said.

She nodded.

"Take the camera home. Make sure it's kept in a safe place, because in a while those pictures will be all that's left of me. They're like those oh-bit-choo-aries—only much more. A person is more than facts. We are every moment we have ever existed on earth, even if none of those moments really counted for anything in the scheme of human progress, even if it was only the last moments we made worth living. You helped me do that, Carrie-Ann. You've given me proof that I was here and that someone shared my triumph with me—triumph over the spitefulness of human memory." He mussed her hair. "I'm glad you came. But you have to go now. Take the camera and leave."

But Carrie-Ann remained, blinking up at him.

"Time to ditch," he said, and walked away. She watched him cross the room. When he turned from the closet on the other side he was holding a snake—not a snake, she realized, but a rope, a thick one with a loop at the end. He clutched it with a trembling hand. "Please, Carrie-Ann. You have to play the game by the rules now. Take Gravity with you… okay?"

She watched him toss the rope over the crossbeam, pulling the knots tight. Shakily, like a pirate forced to walk the plank, he climbed to the top of the stool.

Carrie-Ann turned away. Behind her, the stepstool made a triumphant, ugly sound as it fulfilled its special purpose. Gravity meowed to her from the top of the stairs; sweeping it in her arms she went down to the living room, where she huddled on the sofa, stroking the cat.

For a long while she listened to the patter of the rain, the ticking of the clock. Then, to nothing at all.

It was dark when she sat up. Streetlight filtered in. Gravity was nowhere in sight. She got down off the couch and mounted the stairs in the vestibule next to the dining room. The landing was shrouded in gloom.

Upstairs, feeling along the wall, treading softly, she thought of a predator stalking its prey, some rarely glimpsed beast of the forest hiding out there in the dark. Up ahead was its stronghold, dim light spilling from the door.

Inside, Lionel dangled in the light slanting in through the small round window, Gravity at his feet, waiting patiently as if at any moment he might unfasten himself and come down. He resembled a hideous scarecrow, head cocked, eyes bulging, lips like a crushed flower.

Cheezoids, she thought, picking up the cat.

THE WIND KICKED UP, sending up a chorus of chimes and filling her nostrils with the scent of wet lawns. A thrill ran through her like a white kitten purring in her six-year-old hands. There were so many fine houses all around, so many grand things to look at. And so many strange people out tonight! Children mostly, though not all, dressed as ghouls and witches and goblins and devils, their costumes so convincing, so real, she had to fight down the urge to flee whenever one of their processions drew near.

She watched them move from door to door, watched hands emerge from doorways to drop candies in their outstretched bags. A group of them drifted to the door of the house she had her eye on.

When they had completed the mysterious ritual Carrie-Ann took their place. She stared a moment at the paper scarecrow hung next to the door.

Ding-dong.

An old woman answered.

"Yes?"

She was as old as anyone Carrie-Ann had ever seen. Her face had as many lines as wrinkles in a tree and a mole on her cheek the size of a raspberry. She was tall and gaunt and withered, like a scarecrow herself. "Come in, come in," she said, throwing open the door. "You'll die of cold." Yet it was the woman's hands that felt cold, like twig stems frozen over; Carrie-Ann was glad to be free of them once she was inside.

She ran her eyes over the magazines and knitting, the photo albums and bookshelves and needlepoint on the walls. The air was musty and smelled of toast. A radio rambled in one corner.

"That poor creature you've got there is thin as a ghost," the woman said, bustling off into another room. "And you... do you live in the neighborhood? I don't believe I've seen you around here. That's a beautiful dress, but you might as well be naked. I'll see if I can find you an old shirt or something. Here's something for the cat..."

When the old woman returned the cat was sitting before the front door, twitching its tail. She laid the bowl on the floor and started when she saw the camera at her feet. It was one of those shiny compact digital ones, the kind her grandson had shown her how to use last week. She bent to pick it up—then realized she was alone in the room.

The old woman stuck her head out the door. There was no one on the street but a man walking his dog and a child in a white sheet toddling after its mother. Some parents that poor girl must have, she thought, shivering, to let her out on Halloween by herself, in nothing but that flimsy dress; it was terrible, so terrible to be alone.

An icy wind breathed into her veins, chilled the bones in her feet. She started to go inside. For an instant her heart lightened when she heard a doorbell ring; she realized it was wind chimes, all the wind chimes of the neighborhood singing.

INSIDIOUS IN THE MONTH OF JUNE

Green-eyed and blind, the diaphanously clad girl turned from the fire as the Lord of Insidiousness entered. She nodded, smiling, as his fingers closed on a fold of silk.

Stunned, he drew back in the moonbeam that slanted perpetually through his window, clutching his bloody cheek.

"Beware the month of June," the girl said, pointing to the calendar by the door, "for you, it is the month of death." Then she was gone.

A gray cat yawned by the hearth and licked its lips; then it, too, was gone.

He died, always, with a look of surprise on his face, as if seeing a sunrise for the first time. Locking himself in, he decreed that all suspects were to take up residence at the front gate, where, mounted on footmen's pikes, they were to greet visitors from the neck up. A blind crone was the first to join the newly formed hospitality committee; in the town square, a scholar was disemboweled for keeping a gray cat.

Delirious with fever, his Lordship sat in his chair and

counted the twenty-eight X's marked in his own hand beneath a grinning skull. Make that twenty-nine, he thought, pitching forward onto the floor.

On the thirtieth day, he was summoned to dine in his own hall.

"Now, what —" He started, then gaped at the woman at the head of his table.

She must have weighed over five hundred pounds. As she feasted, her soiled bib swayed and heaved with the rhythm of her bosom like abstract art painted on a ship's sail. With a cat's reflexes she swiped a dish of mutton. Her eyes flicked up to him, barely more than green-centered slits in the doughy bulges of her circling cheeks.

"Is that you?" He asked, sitting next to her.

"It's closer than what you saw earlier."

He spread his hands in the air. "What is this?"

"We're celebrating." She licked her thumb and forefinger clean. "A well-deserved transition into the next life or oblivion, whichever takes you. Lazy man's suicide, I call it."

"What are you?"

"My name's Judith."

In his memories of another life, two hands clapped. "The nurse!"

"Nurse's aide."

"How are you here?"

"You'll have to read my mind for that information."

"How did you disable my avatar?"

"By reading yours."

"Right."

She shrugged. "It's true. Not all registered telepaths end up in intelligence. I consider myself a student of human nature."

"And why should I interest you?"

"Just like a man," the Nurse-Judith-Glutton said, in a theatrical aside. She plucked up a goblet of wine, quaffed it, slammed it on the table. "Because I'm sick of making my rounds and hearing the vulgar, egocentric thoughts that buzz in your heads while you wait for the cryo folks to disconnect you and take you to the organ farm. It's disgusting. It's just plain selfish."

"Say whatever you like."

"Do you believe in an afterlife?"

His eyes narrowed. He stuffed a grape in his mouth.

"I'm told I have nine months left to live," she continued, and smoothed the tablecloth on either side of her plate. "Cancer. I found out one year ago, a year to the day after my husband died of the same. But we'll see if I succumb to the suggestive power of experts who devalue their patients as quickly as he did."

She snorted.

"Anyway, unlike my husband, I decided to make the most of however much time I have left. I took a cruise in the Mediterranean. I wrote some poems. I painted my house and climbed Mount Hood. The final item on my to-do list was to talk one perfectly healthy specimen from taking advantage of the euthanaut clinics because he's afraid of life, not death."

Her eyes darted from side to side, and she leaned in, continued: "I always hated those places. They're like funeral homes for the dead-to-be. They smell of two-thirds disinfectant and one-third sanctimoniousness. The doctors look like used car salesmen. And every few minutes one of you moans with pleasure, rolling in whatever flavor-of-the-month fantasy you've selected. Eighty-five percent of the patients are male, you know."

"I'm sorry you have cancer," he said, and popped another grape in his mouth, "but I think you're being unfair."

"On the contrary. I sympathize with you. I lost most of my sight in a car accident when I was twenty-five. Suicide —real suicide, the kind that hurts—entered my mind on occasion, but slashing my wrist or throwing myself off a bridge wasn't going to solve anything. People counted on me, as they do on you. Time to be Jeremy Gray again, retired contractor."

"I have no children," he said.

"Doesn't matter."

"How do you nurse us when you're blind?"

"My nerves were affected, not my eyes. Doctors still can't sort it out. I see things, just differently."

"I'll say. And you can read—"

"*That* was the whim of nature. And now it's your turn. I asked you earlier if you believed in an afterlife. Well?"

He nibbled on a fig and sat back, folding his hands on his stomach.

"I see where you're going with this. The blind girl act wasn't just because you really are blind, was it, any more than the, uh, heavier person you are now reflects that you're morbidly obese in real life. You want me to see what you believe is a form of cowardice—namely my presence at the clinic—and you want me to witness the grotesqueness of my indulgence. Well, what I do here is my business, my intellectual property, paid for in full. You have no right to interfere."

"There's no privacy law concerning telepathic intrusion in a euthanaut clinic," she countered, with, he thought, a note of disdain.

"It's still my fantasy," he said. He helped himself to a decanter of brandy.

"If only you could see it from my point of view. The lot of you men, immersed in your horny dreamscapes, your atrophying bodies the flesh-and-bone equivalent of Dorian Gray's picture. At least most of my women patients *do* things: They fly jumbo jets, or walk the stage as concert pianists, or invent a mathematical formula that solves world hunger. Men are either Sir Lancelot or the Marquis de Sade. You could go to a quickjack deck for what you're after."

"You don't know at all what I'm after."

Her face, for all its pink, greasy folds, hardened. "Perhaps you don't know the distinction between intuition and ESP, mister. I don't need the first to read you, and I barely need the second. She did the dishes, didn't she?"

"What?"

"And ironed your shirts."

"What has that got to do with it?"

"My husband made great pizza meatloaf. I don't know anyone who makes a great pizza meatloaf anymore. It's one of those things I took for granted. And to think I was told I have no future… well, I do. Before I resign I'm going to see one of you noodle-heads checks out of this place, sinks his teeth in real beef and cheese, or vegan beef and cheese if that's what you want, not this pseudo-historical fluff that belongs in some old Camelot B-movie. *That* is my future.

"I really don't mean to belittle your loss," she continued, reaching for an éclair. "But tough love, here: Life is always hard, isn't it? Why, at fifty-five, should you decide it's not worth it? And who are you to decide?"

"That," Jeremy said, straightening with his hands on the table, "is a discussion for politicians and legislators."

"Then let's get back to my earlier question. Do you believe in an afterlife?"

He sighed.

"I believe in doing nothing. Whether or not I'm aware of it makes no difference to me."

A frown tugged at her marshmallow cheeks. Still chewing on the éclair, she reached for the peach cobbler.

Ever the gentleman, the Lord of Insidiousness slid it within reach.

With all the quickness of her earlier food-snatching, the Nurse-Judith-Glutton seized his wrist. Her grip dug in like a steel claw. He shot her a questioning glance. Her head looked like it was about to explode, the flesh flushed and beaded with sweat, the eyes like puckered navels, not even the whites visible through the quivering flesh around them.

"You disgust me," she said, spraying custard.

"Why? What did I say?"

"You're worse than lazy—you have no commitments, no beliefs whatsoever. You truly have no reason to live."

"You're upset," he said, tugging at his hand without success, "because you see me wasting the gift of life that is being threatened in your case. I get that. But abusing me in my own fantasy—a fantasy I paid for—isn't going to reverse our situations."

"You piss on the question of an afterlife."

"I don't believe in God, I'm clinically depressed and I have a right to piss on the afterlife."

"You have no rights!"

At first he thought she smiled. A mad woman's smile,

yes. Then he realized it was her mouth spreading open. Wide. And wider.

"Let me go, Judith." Was he really talking to an infuriated, blind, telepathic nurse's aide at his bedside?

"I sentence you to your final death in the tradition of Castle Jeremy," she said. Not the nurse's glutton avatar, he realized, but the gray cat, wagging its tail at the foot of the table. It added:

"I'm giving you an afterlife whether you believe in one or not."

The mouth of the mighty woman grew as wide as the face that possessed it. The face was like a rubber band of flesh, or several all tangled in each other, stretching to make way for an enormous finger. A finger made of gums, lips, tongue and teeth. Yellow teeth. Bad breath. Hot.

Jeremy steamrolled over the plate of peach cobbler, caught in her iron grip. His last thought, as he rode up her bosom and peered into her gaping maw was: At least I'll wake up back in my room.

THE SUN, a bloody jewel, was about to set. Jagged mountain peaks, drunk on the last spills of rose light, parted for its passing. God, be done with it already, thought the Lord of Insidiousness, gazing on his former lands. Then he noticed figures winding across the plain in a sluggish, defeated fashion.

Under the never-quite-setting-sun (she savored uncertainties) he watched them pick their way among the rocks. The ones in front wore torn, soiled garments, their hands and feet bound in chains. A number of tall, brawny figures prodded at them with axe heads and spears.

Jeremy put on his most regal smile as they approached.

"Good evening, sir," said a red-headed captive, raising a hand while he caught his breath, "we are commanded to greet someone outside the castle wall. It appears you alone are in any condition to return the courtesy."

"Welcome to Castle Jeremy," Jeremy croaked, his tongue dry as leather.

It looked like the aftermath of Hell Week gathered before him. Togas hung in shreds from most of the men, though a few looked dressed for a science fiction convention and one wore a Confederate soldier's uniform. Their captors grunted in what sounded like pig squeals played backward.

"No offense, but it does not look quite welcoming," the man said. "In fact, I wonder your master can enjoy himself in such a place at all."

"I have not seen the inside myself in some time," Jeremy confessed.

This brought chuckles all around, and more squeals from the captors.

"Pardon us, sir," said the man, "we make not light of you. I should explain the situation. Each of us, it seems, was summoned to your lands. Indeed, we found ourselves in pitched battle against this band of devils for no reason we can discern. It appears we are your prisoners."

"Castle Jeremy does not take prisoners," Jeremy said.

"We know that, sir. That is why we laugh."

"I am Jeremy Stormblade, Lord of Insidiousness, Haunted Warrior-Poet and Bloodthirsty Prince."

"And I am Erik the Deep, Tormentor of Maidenhood. On my right is Gil the Elusive, and on my left is Augustus Ironthew, he of the Black Glove. The rest of this company are fine men all. I take it you are master of this estate. You do not know, then, what has brought us here?"

He wondered. Had Nurse's Aide Judith really entered the minds of the male patients and coerced them into this reimagining of his once idyllic world—this feminist satire of the Knights of the Round Table? Was there a nurse's aide named Judith, or had he invented her, hungry for antagonism in a dreamworld void of drama?

Perhaps terrorists had hacked into the euthanaut mainframe, infecting the machines with a neurovirus like the one they'd used in Cancun. The tourists all went mad, he recalled.

"You'll love the sunsets here," he said.

The first axe fell.

THE NECROMANCER'S GUIDE TO POSITIVE SELF-TALK

THE MAN WAS KILLED ON A NIGHT LIKE THIS. THE ENDLESS prairie ghostly with frost and the cries of wolves sheltering from the moon.

How he hated that deep red orb hanging high above the town of Ever Gleaming. Its blotchy surface reminded him of the scars under his sheepskin vest and blue shirt. "That is no moon," Old Ben had said, and the preacher had been right, in a sense the man had learned the hard way. For the unheavenly body cast a profane refulgence over the byway that linked the Western lands to the underworld.

The animals knew this. The indigenous peoples knew this. Only the white settlers refused to run from the War Moon's malefic glow. Instead, the man's betrayers huddled throughout the town with unwavering confidence in the pistoleers they had engaged for the deadliest night in three years. As if ten Union ex-soldiers would stand a chance against the monsters when the War Moon grew its biggest and bloodiest.

The man sipped his coffee and went back into the log cabin.

Seated at the dining table, he watched the hired guns through the open door. Not since he had gone by the name Burbank had winter's chains burdened his bones. Only nightmares troubled him anymore—and even these had become less a cause for alarm than an object of study.

Now, when the man traveled to Morpheus's domain, he felt clear and alert to the horrors he revisited from his past life. An unknown agency drove him to dig deep into his slumbering visions, even deeper than the underground burial chamber it had helped him escape. Although, help is too nice a word, probably.

I mean, would you want to return from the dead to save a town full of dickbags who let you get eaten by giant, man-eating rabbits?

Exactly. And the man didn't, either. But the agency kept him on the path to Ever Gleaming and the reckoning it required.

Anyway, he looked forward to paying back the bunnies from Hell. If dreams held the key to revenge, then he would gladly perish in the theater of sleep until he pinpointed his archenemy's weakness.

The man clenched his fist upon the table.

"Tonight," he said, in a voice like winter wind rushing over cowards' graves. "This ends tonight. In filth. In torment. In long-eared, cuddly-looking things getting shot to pieces. Oh, yes. I am finishing this. I am the Finisher of Foul and Unjust Situations."

But that's a weird, awkward title, isn't it? Instead, let's call the man... *the Whispering Gunslinger.*

"Tonight," the Whispering Gunslinger said. "Tonight, I

send Vito and the Binky gang back to their infernal maker."

"IT IS TIME."

The Whispering Gunslinger gulped down cold coffee dregs and stood. He had watched the gunmen long enough to predict they would fall by their faith in human invention.

Judging by their positions throughout the town, they expected to defeat the outlaws again with the Gatling gun they had employed in the previous conflict. They had no way of knowing they had caught the Binky siblings at a low point in their shapeshifting career, with their leader absent and little nourishment available from the energetically dull Pumpkin Moon.

When the marauders attacked this time, the gunmen would find a very different gang with a War Moon in the sky and Branson Vito—recently escaped from federal prison—leading the charge. Lagomorphically enhanced, the bandit chief would be even crueler, stronger, and hungrier than when he had mobilized the first raid on Ever Gleaming. By unhappy coincidence, he fancied himself a student of the black arts and knew that tonight would grant him more potency than he had accessed in ages.

"But he does not know about me."

The Whispering Gunslinger took his gun belt off the wall.

"My instruments bear the sigils of vengeance." He belted the Colts around him and stroked their detailed mother-of-pearl inlays. "My hands are quick." He jerked the revolvers out and pointed them at the open door. "My bullets fly true." He spun the guns, tossed them in a juggler's exchange and thrust them back into their holsters. "My words forge the sword of truth." Reverently, as if performing a ritual as old as human suffering, he donned his black, woolen poncho and wide-brimmed hat —both patterned with the symbols on his gun grips.

"I am the Finisher of Foul and Unjust Situations," he said.

He scowled.

"I mean, I am the Whispering Gunslinger. And tonight, I whisper… retribution."

HIS FINAL PREPARATION was to burn the book: *The Necromancer's Guide to Positive Self-Talk.*

He had found it in his niche at the back of the underground burial chamber along with the six-shooters, poncho, and hat. Without question, he had taken these mysterious bestowals with him into a valley far from Ever Gleaming and learned the sorcerer's methods of internal dialogue.

From the grimoire, he had learned the spells for banishing negative perceptions. He had memorized the runes for redirecting harmful thoughts. He had honed his concentration to wield the transcendental gun. Now, on the eve of battle, he stood ready to perform the final step to adeptship:

"Whosoever mastereth the arms and armature of Spectral Avengement shall cast this book into the flames of Absolute Will."

He took the spellbook from the mantel and tossed it into the hearth.

"I thank thee for thy wisdom," he said, watching the leather bindings catch fire. "And for the victory you doth give me on this night."

The Whispering Gunslinger walked out of the log cabin.

He descended the hill overlooking the town. A hush lay across the frosted prairie. The gunmen should have read the wolves' silence as a sign that Hell was about to open. Instead, they smoked pipes and exchanged banter occasionally, swollen with pride in the technological terror that Dr. Richard J. Gatling had created. Unless they came to their senses, they would serve better as diversions than brothers-in-arms when Vito led his furry abominations into the town.

The Binkies. Chuck, Morgan, Josey, and Sim. Under the War Moon, the werebunny bandits would hand Colonel Lowell Magnum a bloodbath unlike any he had seen on the killing grounds of Virginia or Tennessee.

"Unless I can stop them." The Whispering Gunslinger glanced at the dirt and rocks heaped at the hill's base. Three years ago, he had burrowed through a similar mound to escape the vault where the dead were stored during the winter.

"And I can. I will—"

"Come a little closer, mister. Hands up so I can see them. Apologies for my brusqueness, but go on, do it."

The shout came from shadows some fifty paces ahead. The Whispering Gunslinger raised his hands and moved slowly across the dirt field. When he had come to within ten paces of the town's main street, the voice told him to stop.

The pistoleers had made a formal entrance with two covered wagons set end to end with enough room for a stagecoach to pass between them. The left wagon's side said BE KIND while the right wagon's side said OR ELSE. Torches mounted on hitching posts illuminated the painted black greeting.

"We wondered when you would come down out of that house," the voice said, from behind the left wagon.

"I did not want to alarm you," the Whispering Gunslinger said.

"What was that?"

"I said I did not want to alarm you."

"Try that again?"

"I said I did not want to alarm you."

"He said he did not want to—"

"I heard him this time," the speaker admonished someone behind the right wagon. "So give me your name, sir, please, and what brings you to this corner of the wasteland. And kindly project your words, for my hearing is none the better for my sojourns in the South."

"I am the Finisher of Foul and Unjust Situations."

"The what?"

"I mean, I am the—"

"He is the Finisher of Foul and Unjust Situations," the second speaker said.

"And is that what you think we have here?" The first speaker stepped into the torch light. He was a burly, goateed man in a tan frock coat and smoked a curved Meerschaum pipe. "A foul and unjust situation? Well, you may be right. But only one man oversees the welfare of the good citizens of Ever Gleaming, and he is I—Colonel Lowell Magnum. Might be that you have heard of me."

"I am aware of your exploits, Colonel. But there is something you too should be aware of."

"Say that again?"

"He said—"

"Oh, let us move on." The colonel gestured toward the Whispering Gunslinger's waist. "Disarm yourself, sir, and toss the guns my way. Slowly and gently, now."

The Whispering Gunslinger said, "They see what I want them to see," and pantomimed the act without surrendering the weapons.

"I thank you." Colonel Magnum grabbed the belt that wasn't really there and puffed on his pipe. "Now, join me for a drink, if you will."

The gunman signaled to his associate behind the other wagon. A sharp-eyed man in a black frock coat joined him in the torch light. "Keep a watch out here, J.W., while our soft-spoken guest and I have a word at the Double Gravy."

"Vito and his outlaws will be here any minute, Colonel," J.W. said.

"We shall drink in haste. All right, young man, come along with me. And welcome to our humble little town."

THE WHISPERING GUNSLINGER passed through the makeshift entrance and followed the colonel.

As they walked down Main Street, he pretended not to notice the hat brims and rifle barrels showing above the redly lit parapets. He took equal care ignoring the elbows and boots stirring in dark alleyways, ruddied by moonlight. What a different town Ever Gleaming had become from the one he remembered. The "good citizens" had turned it into a principality ruled by Civil War veterans, whose needs had led to a private hotel with its own saloon, stable, and brothel.

In turn, the hired guns maintained a guard tower and a strict code of conduct, making for an orderly haven from outlaws and monsters disguised as outlaws.

Speaking of which, the Whispering Gunslinger said, "You are mine, Vito, you and your minions. You will die by my command of the transcendental gun."

"Well, you are one for susurration," Colonel Magnum said, and pointed his pipe at the Double Gravy's batwing doors. "Let us susurrate over some whiskey inside my office."

Inside the dim saloon, under the gaze of stuffed deer heads and paintings of nude women, the Whispering Gunslinger brooded at a table while the colonel poured drinks behind the bar.

"Now then." Colonel Magnum set the glasses on the table and pulled up a chair. "From the look on your face, I would guess you have been through these parts before."

"Your town looks like a place I once called home."

"Forgive my suspicious nature. But then, that is how I have built a refuge from the barbarians who roam the wasteland these days. Ever Gleaming has no sheriff, you know."

"I noticed that."

"Yes, you would have." The colonel sipped his whiskey and shut his eyes a moment. "By Jiminy, this Sweaty Scrotum is aptly named, but if you give it a few seconds, I swear there is a payoff."

The Whispering Gunslinger knocked back his drink.

"A hint of maple sugar with a smoky aftertaste and a bit of zing on the mouth," he said.

"And a trace of boot leather, would you say? Anyway, to business, for, as my chief assistant implied, you have caught us on a troublesome night." The colonel leaned his elbow on the table and made an interrogative gesture with his pipe. "My line of work compels me to ask, sir, why you were spying on us from the empty house on the hill… and why you would be so obvious about it."

"I wanted you to see the fire burning, Colonel, so you would not feel threatened when I approached the town entrance. I wanted you to know that I am not your enemy."

"Then what is your interest in our affairs? What do the people of Ever Gleaming have to do with the situation you seek to rectify?"

"Those are complicated questions. However, I can narrow the answers down to this: I know you are preparing to do battle with the Binkies and their leader, Branson Vito, who may or may not be known to you. I also know you hope to defeat them with the strategy you used during your previous clash with the bandits. Unfortunately, my sources tell me your plan will backfire tonight."

"Who are your sources?"

"I wish I could tell you. I have no answer."

Colonel Magnum puffed on his pipe. "And how can a Gatling gun fail against a gaggle of oversized, pugnacious rabbits?"

"I believe the proper word is 'fluffle,'" the Whispering Gunslinger said. "A fluffle of oversized, pugnacious rabbits. Anyway, your Gatling gun will not work against Branson Vito, Colonel. Even under a common full moon, he possesses more strength than all the Binkies combined. That strength increases unpredictably when a War Moon arises. Tonight, we are seeing a War Moon greater than any that has occurred in eons. Your firepower will not save the town this time."

The colonel grunted. "A full moon is still just a moon.

Tonight's is no different from any other, although I will grant you that ruddy coin in the sky has an arresting quality."

"I tell you that is no moon," the Whispering Gunslinger said. "Not in the usual sense."

"You do realize we are dealing with rabbits, do you not?"

"Technically, they are therianthropic—"

"Big ones that start as people and resume that dubious status when the moon wanes. Granted, these lagomorph hybrids are celestially powered, but the extent depends on personal predisposition, not a slew of optical phenomena… if that is what you are suggesting. The same applies to werewolves and wereraccoons and the like."

"Your gun will not work," the Whispering Gunslinger insisted.

"I think it will, sir. I have seen Dr. Gatling's peacekeeper in action. From an offensive standpoint, I would say it is the ultimate power in the universe, for nothing resolves an antagonism like a dragon breathing fire two-hundred times in a minute. We will prevail over the rabbits again, that I guarantee. Although, your sympathizing is appreciated, however mystifying and misguided."

Boot heels thudding on the boardwalk made them look toward the batwing doors.

"The Binkies are closing in from the north, Colonel," J.W. said, peeking in.

"I will join you, directly," Colonel Magnum said, and stood.

"Well, young fellow, you are an odd stick, as they say. But your conversation has stimulated me. And it gives me confidence that you will, if nothing else, respect my authority on the field of battle tonight. You may take your guns from the bar. I presume you have skill with them, based on your intrepid style of vagabondage. In fact, if you were to play a supportive role in the foul and unjust situation that is about to descend upon us, I would happily refill your glass of Sweaty Scrotum in our moment of triumph."

"I would be honored."

"Only… get down when you hear Old Agatha breathing fire from the schoolhouse. She has a strong opinion regarding these hare-brained, moon-muddled fluffle runners."

"Technically, Colonel, they are rabbit-brained, not hare-brained."

"By Jiminy, you are precise."

FROM THE DOUBLE Gravy's balcony, the Whispering Gunslinger watched himself die.

Like a spectator in one of his dreams, he saw his mangled form thrash in the water trough in front of Doc Baumeister's office. He saw the Binkies hop about him, taking turns with the viscera spilling from his sundered belly. He heard Sheriff Lee's Winchester discharge from inside Burbank & Sons General Store.

Then he watched as Branson Vito, in human form, ordered the monsters to make way. Bullets glanced off the outlaw's moonlight-armored back as he sauntered toward the broken thing in the water trough. While his lackeys leaped back and forth in the crimson light, Vito pushed the young shopkeeper under the water and sloshed him around. When he pulled his arm from the overflowing bath, he held up a dark, meaty clump.

I know, too obvious, right? But that's what Branson Vito did—he ripped out Jim Burbank's heart.

Leaning on the balcony rail, the Whispering Gunslinger reflected on the vision that might have been hilariously cliché had it not happened right in front of him, not to mention *to* him, down on the street. If only it had yielded the memory, the clue to Vito's chink in the armor, which his dreams had also withheld.

"But it will come to me," he said, gripping the top rail so hard he pried a chunk loose. "For nothing escapes the Finisher of Foul and Unjust—that is, nothing escapes the Whispering Gunslinger."

He turned his attention to the smoke puffs in the north. Three years ago, the Cheyenne had apprised the town of the shapeshifters, but the miners had dismissed the warning as bosh. For their skepticism, seven courageous men had paid the price, including Sheriff Lee, Jim Burbank, and Old Ben the preacher, while the townspeople cowered from the wererabbit bandits in every nook and cranny.

Too bad more men would pay tonight for Colonel Magnum's skepticism.

Not that his dismissive attitude came as a surprise. How could the ex-soldier be persuaded to suspend everything he knew about warfare? How could he be convinced that superior combat power meant nothing in the present arena? To compound the problem, war, whiskey, and whoremongering had hardened his philosophy to the point that even hulking, carnivorous bunnies failed to strike him as symptoms of a darkness vaster than any earthly battleground.

"Enemy spotted," a voice shouted from the guard tower. "They look even nastier than they were before. And there's a fifth one bringing up the rear… he must be as big as a buffalo!"

"This is it, men," the colonel thundered, racing toward the schoolhouse. "Strike swiftly and fearlessly!"

"For the boys at Antietam," someone shouted.

"For the people of Ever Gleaming," another cried.

The gunmen motivated each other for the contest ahead. The Whispering Gunslinger nodded.

Now, he made out the enemy. The deadly fluffle curved westward, flanked by Cheyenne archers on horseback. They headed off the wererabbit bandits, diverting them toward an alleyway that gave on to the town's center. Though these were daring men, they had likely been paid from the same coffer that treated the white mercenaries like princes. The riders made sure Vito followed his minions into the alleyway, then galloped into the night.

Crammed into the passageway, the Binkies took fire from the rooftops. Vito jumped over them and hopped into the main street. With his hind leg, he kicked over a Prairie Schooner. Then with both hind legs, he sent the wagon flying like a giant brick into the empty Sheriff's Office. The charmed arrows in his back made him ornery.

Vito's gesture spurred the marauders to force their way to the main street. One didn't need to be a mysteriously informed Spectral Avenger to see these were not the same Binkies who had terrorized the town previously. With a War Moon heightening their powers and Vito setting the pace, they aimed to bring utter devastation to the streets. Tonight's raid would be a massacre, not a glorified food run.

Keep in mind these were *therianthropes*, lunar transmutations of humans into beasts. At full moonrise, even kindly shapeshifters succumbed to their worst instincts... and the Binkies were not given to kindly acts, not even in two-legged form. Between them, they had shot or killed over a hundred men, not counting the time Sim shot a girl in the foot for giggling at his mustache. I mention this to save time describing buildings tumbling and blood turning the frosted ground an even deeper crimson than the moonlight.

Ever Gleaming was about to become a pile of bones and kindling—a prospect that negated Colonel Magnum's privileges as defense chief.

At least, that's how the Whispering Gunslinger saw it.

"Now, I join the fray," he said, vaulting over the rail (he could talk and do gymnastics simultaneously) and landing on Chuck's back as the black werebunny bandit rammed a corner post of the building next to the Double Gravy. His preternatural ability to distinguish the fluffy ruffians made vengeance all the sweeter. "Now, I invoke the transcendental gun."

Clutching prairie-dusted fur, the Whispering Gunslinger pulled a charmed arrow from the creature's spine and knifed it deep into the wound. At the same time, his otherworldly Colts flew from under his poncho, spun in mid-air and spat death at chocolate-eared Morgan racing past in the other direction. Chuck stumbled and slid to a stop outside the general store while the other Binky hopped in circles. Finally, Morgan collapsed beside the water trough where Jim Burbank had relinquished his heart to Branson Vito.

"Vito."

Standing astride Chuck's carcass, the Whispering

Gunslinger spread his poncho to make room for his flying revolvers.

"You should have attacked me while my six-shooters were preoccupied," he taunted his unseen nemesis.

He turned his attention to Josey.

The blue steel behemoth eyed its prey from a wreckage of broken wagons, barrels, and timbers. Its ears pointed down and its teeth showed bright red stains. It stomped its hind feet and charged. The Whispering Gunslinger tossed his hat in the air and drew the revolvers, striking the target with three rounds from each Colt. When the hat dropped halfway, six bullets burst from the crown and tore into Josey's enraged werebunny brain. The monster fell on its side, snarled and grew still.

The Whispering Gunslinger jumped down from Chuck's scruff and swept up his Swiss-cheese remnant of hat.

THREE BINKIES DOWN.

Nine gunmen slain.

One colonel gone missing.

Only Vito and Sim remained.

The Whispering Gunslinger tossed his weapons into the street. He looked at the wooden wall sealing off the town's northwest corner. Built next to Old Ben's cabin, it formed the cul-de-sac where the colonel had hoped to trap the marauders and gun them down with Old Agatha.

So much for repeating victory with the ultimate power in the universe. Now, instead of ex-Union marksmen manning the parapet, Sim stood on the barrier, sniffing the War Moon's mélange of dust, gun smoke, and blood. The monster made no move when it spotted its siblings' killer, only regarded him with baleful ruby eyes. The Whispering Gunslinger pointed his right trigger finger at Sim and made a raspy sound in the back of his throat.

The last Binky glanced at the guns in the street. Then it thumped its hind feet on the walkway and hopped onto Old Ben's slanted rooftop. Wagging its barely discernible tail, the huge, white puffball jumped from sight.

"Well, now, who would you be, Cap'n, who shows such doughtiness against the nastiest, beastliest werebunny bandits of the wasteland?"

The Whispering Gunslinger turned. Twenty paces away, near Morgan's carcass, Branson Vito faced him.

And yes, Vito's verbal style sounds suspiciously like Colonel Magnum's, but the outlaw had read a lot of books while in prison. Besides, what better time to turn some fancy phrases than in a showdown among ravaged buildings, gunfighters' corpses, and wererabbit carcasses?

Presumably for speech-giving purposes, Vito presented himself in human form. Unlike most shapeshifters, he controlled his transformations during a full moon. The outlaw cut a dashing figure for someone who had ripped apart four men and eaten his own feces minutes earlier (autocoprophagy persisting as a lagomorph behavior among therianthropes). He wore a black hat and duster coat—pierced by a dozen arrows—over matching clothes and carried grime in an evenly distributed way, so that he looked rugged, and not like some laborer who never washed hands after using the outhouse.

Although, did people wash their hands in the Old West? No matter. Vito looked sharp with his artful scruffiness and lazy half-smile, a true fallen angel at home on the dark side of the gun and moon as well, loosely speaking.

The Whispering Gunslinger wondered if he had under-estimated his opponent.

"I am the Finisher..." He cleared his throat. "I mean, I have come here to finish a foul and unjust situation."

Vito thought a moment and snorted. "Foul and unjust? And what about the cannon that shredded my gang the last time they passed through here? And what about you, Cap'n, with your mental style of gunplay, succeeding where the warmongers failed?"

"My designation is epithetical, not hierarchical. I am—"

"You are either getting over a cold or have a fondness for shout-whispering. But more importantly... you are in a difficulty, Cap'n."

"I wish you would stop calling me that."

"Now, I grant you, you have special powers. Your weapons do not come from this world. But my weapons come from even *more* not this world. Wait. I can do better than that." The bandit frowned. "My weapons come... they are even... damn it, you get the point. Speaking of guns, I saw your colonel lighting a shuck for the hills. He has abandoned you—which leaves you fighting alone for a herd of pusillanimous nincompoops who will not come to your aid, not even to save themselves."

Vito held out his hand.

"Tell you what, Cap'n. It could be that you have only begun to discover your power. Join my gang, and together we can rule the country as leader and Binky replacement."

The Whispering Gunslinger lifted his poncho. His guns floated down into their holsters.

"So be it," Vito said. He made a fist. When he unclenched it, a spinning wheel of green electricity appeared in his palm. "If you will not replace my Binky kin, you will join them. A shame, because with our combined strength, we could have brought ineffable mayhem to the Western territories. Although, I get to show off my progress in the black arts, so there is that."

Bowing his head, he struck a first-rate evil sorcerer's pose.

With a flick of his wrist, Vito sent the disk streaking toward the one person brave enough to challenge him. The hate-charged energy struck the Whispering Gunslinger like a lightning bolt. He dropped to his knees, holding in exposed guts while his flesh smoked and sparked.

"But you were supposed to die by my command…" He fell face-first into the ground without finishing his sentence. The frost melted around him.

Vito chuckled. "What can I say? You are not the only one who can mentally manipulate the elements, Cap'n. I had ample time to develop my talents in the calaboose." He glanced at his toady watching from the parapet again. "I must confess, cousin Sim, that was a gratifying test of my present abilities. But what do you say we get on with the banquet? Without the others, we shall have—"

"Well, Branson Vito, do you have any last words before you suffer the vitriol of Old Agatha?"

The bandit looked up, gape-mouthed. Some fifteen feet overhead, the speaker circled him in an upside-down-T-shaped contraption kept aloft by a rotating blade fixed to its mast. Made from wood and steel, the machine looked like a drunkenly conceived imitation of a prehistoric bird. A ludicrous thing to take into battle, and yet it gave its navigator a flexible vantage point behind the Gatling gun mounted on the front of the wooden bed. A man in his fifties, he looked both boyish and gentlemanly, dangling his legs over the sides and smoking a pipe.

"Colts that self-fire and a cannon that flies," Vito marveled.

"Tonight's events have not transpired according to my design," the man said. "I am afraid I underestimated you and your gang, sir."

"You must be Colonel Magnum." Vito turned his head as the flying cannon arced past him again. Unfortunately for Vito's neck, the colonel enjoyed expatiating even more than he did.

"I had meant to trap you all in front of the school-house," Colonel Magnum expatiated, "so you would antic-ipate the same ace in the hole I had used previously. Then… *da-da-da-da-da-da-da-da*!—death from above. That would have been quite the killing blow, would you agree? By Jiminy. However, although my plan fell short, I have nevertheless protected my employers and shall hasten your quietus forthwith. Take this point to your grave, Branson Vito: You are exceptional, but not invincible. Now, witness the power of this fully armed and operational Gatling station!"

Old Agatha breathed fire on the Binky chief. As the bullets glanced off him, Vito smiled.

"Impressive, most impressive," he said. "But now it is my turn, Colonel." He made a fist, opened it and revealed a glowing green ball. He flung the energy shell at the Gatling station's tail. The impact blew the vertical piece off the end, condemning the colonel to a fiery death as he rode his technological terror over his saloon and into the field where Old Ben used to preach.

Vito closed his eyes.

"Boom," he said.

Well, not really boom. More like *ppffgggkkkhaagghhh*. Childishly onomatopoetic. But pretty close to the actual explosion noise for someone who had never heard a flying machine crash before, not even on television.

"And now, Sim to the—"

"Wait. I remember, now. I remember."

Slipping and swaying, the Whispering Gunslinger climbed to his feet.

Vito doffed his hat and scratched the top of his ginger-haired head. "By Baal's beard, I am looking forward to being done with this night."

Taking his turn in an evening of expatiating, the Whispering Gunslinger explained his sudden recall. He had been dreaming of Jim Burbank's murder when a minor detail caught his attention, perhaps because he identified so closely with the shopkeeper in his electrocuted, near-death-like state. The incident involved Vito stumbling in horse manure while his minions fed on Burbank.

"'I will have someone's head for this encroachment upon my lizard outsoles,' you shouted," the Whispering Gunslinger shout-whispered. "'No, even better... *I will have someone's heart.*'"

"You make it sound like I gave that promise in a specially slanted typeface, Cap'n," Vito said, showing off his bookish inclinations. "But more to the point, you are implying that you, somehow, are the man who paid for a horse's ass that night."

"You loathe horse pucky, Vito, that is your Achilles's heel. Now that I know it, eat shit and die."

Spreading his hands like an angel of death (which he was, more or less), the Whispering Gunslinger mentally lifted all the equine egesta within a mile and directed it at its harshest detractor.

"*Nnnoooooo!*" Vito cried, in a voice that deserved a specially slanted typeface.

The bandit ducked under the coprological bombardment. The waste of uncounted steeds piled on top of him. Weighed down by the mountain of undigested forage, he could do nothing but wait for the onslaught to stop so he could mentally burst free.

But the chance would never come. For the Whispering Gunslinger, who could not die because he was technically dead, but could depart the earthly plane prematurely, having been resurrected by means known only to the spirit realm, had traveled to the border of the underworld and found self-knowledge akin to godhood in the healing flames of Absolute Will. So said the vanishing gash in his belly and the argent symbols glowing on his gun grips, Swiss-cheese hat, and partially disintegrated poncho.

"I am unstoppable," he said. "I am all-powerful. Well… not all-powerful, but really, really powerful. Powerful enough to put a bullet in you, Branson Vito. Right in your therianthropic, misanthropic heart."

Of course, the bandit couldn't hear the shout-whispered, somewhat alliterative speech, but he must have sensed its import, for he thrust a great fawn forefoot through the fecal encumbrance.

He would have freed himself, too, if the Whispering Gunslinger had not drawn his six-shooter and blasted Vito's emerging werebunny bulk where he said he would.

"Boom," the Whispering Gunslinger said.

Well, not really boom. More like *ppffgggkkkhaagghhh*. A failed attempt at onomatopoeia in this case, but then, who can accurately vocalize an explosion of hundreds of pounds of horse hooey and man-rabbit? Furthermore, who would hope to be heard above the stercoraceous storm of consequence that turned Ever Gleaming into Ever Stinking for the next six months?

"*Ppffkkkoooaaahhhh,*" the Whispering Gunslinger said, coining another puzzling word to punctuate his no-look, over-the-shoulder blasting of Sim. More dung-laden lago-chunks showered down from the parapet.

"And so I win." The shit-spattered avenger spun his glowing Colt, tossed it over his shoulder and caught it behind his back, then reversed the trick and holstered it. "I win through the power of dreams and positive thinking… and horse pucky."

As if in celebration, the wolves resumed howling.

"Hmm… that gives me an idea." Rubbing the scars on his belly, the Whispering Gunslinger ambled toward the overturned wagons marking the town's entrance. "Come out," he called out to the shambles of Main Street. "Show yourselves, you dickbags, or by Abaddon, I will make you eat the stuff I am standing in. I know you hear me, for I have sharpened your aural faculties."

A door creaked open behind him.

From the cul-de-sac enclosing the undamaged school-house, the people of Ever Gleaming straggled toward him.

Well, actually, they weren't people anymore, not in a strict sense. They had become short, fuzzy, shaggy-eared, bright-eyed, two-legged creatures that looked adorable or obnoxiously sweet, depending on your tolerance for anthropomorphically embellished toy dogs.

"Please, sir," one said, in a high-pitched, scratchy voice. "We are begging you—change us back into what we were."

The Whispering Gunslinger scowled. "No way. Before,

you were timid, weak-willed and cowardly. Now, you are tough, valiant and loyal, not to mention almost too cute to gaze upon, except to those who lack whimsy and a tender heart. You may as well accept what you have become." He tilted his head. "You are like the wolves, now. You will look out for each other. You will rebuild your shelter and defend it as one… to the death, if need be. No longer will you suffer oppression under the War Moon or any other lunar influence. That should give you comfort when I am gone."

"Who are you, mister?" A whelp among the dog-like-people asked.

"Someone… who was on your side once." The Whispering Gunslinger turned and headed toward the ruined entrance where the torches still burned.

"Now dance, for you have much to celebrate," he said, over his shoulder.

He faded to nothing within the torches' glow.

"Come back," a young, comparatively nubile dog-like-person shouted tearfully. "Come back, Someone Who Was On Your Side Once, do not abandon us! Please, we need you!"

"No." The elder one who had begged for mercy spun around and clapped his hands to an imaginary beat. "We do not need the man with the soft voice and levitating weapons. For he has bequeathed to us his Absolute Will."

Another swayed and shrugged her shoulders rhythmically. "This is true. Somehow, we have inherited the stranger's determination, grit, and belief in a greater good."

In unison, the dog-like-people said, "From this moment on, we stand together, for we are all Someone Who Was On Your Side Once."

They looked at each other.

"That is, we are all… the Whispering Gunslinger."

And they danced under the bloody moonlight in the muck that would seed an age of solidarity.

And for a thousand years, peace reigned throughout the land, for this story did not happen where you think it did, but in an alternate American West

*A LONG TIME ago in a parallel universe far,
 far away…*

WE ARE OSIRIS AND THE FORTY-TWO JUDGES (TRUTH CANCER!)

ASK MOST PEOPLE HOW THE ANCIENT EGYPTIANS BUILT THE Giza pyramids, and they will tell you the same thing:

"They cheated."

Having heard this sort of opinion before, you will want to press further and ask how ancient Egypt got hold of creatine supplements. But you refrain, for you've seen how historical arguments tend to ignore logistical details. Instead, they churn and bubble over in the virtual vat of *ethics* that has become our dominant means of cultural exchange these days. To settle the pyramid question, it doesn't matter whether creatine was recognized, let alone available, when Khufu and company built their massive monuments; it gave the pharaohs' builders an unfair advantage. And so falls another bygone civilization under the weight of antiquity outrage, as if being conquered by the Roman empire in 30 BC wasn't enough.

But in case you've been out of the history loop lately, the ancient Egyptians are not the only long-dead people to succumb to Internet chastisement. Military leaders in

Ancient China's Warring States Period fell under attack for reportedly distributing beta-alanine and L-citrulline to heavy infantry units. Aztec *ullamaliztli* judges received low scores for allegedly letting ball players prefuel for the big game with potions containing branched-chain amino acids and testosterone boosters. Then there are the Mayans, who fed their own hearts to the Web when outragers started a movement with the claim that executioners took trenbolone (a steroid popular among bodybuilders) to increase their strength for the killing blow.

Thanks to hypermuscular Mayan executioners, we now have #darksidehistory, a meme and movement that roots out every transgression against natural, unassisted physical effort in the ancient world.

Until last year, the ancient times got a pass from pre-twentieth-century history policing. But being the apoplectic leviathan that it is, the outrage culture couldn't resist funneling some of its fury toward antiquity after #effyourmiddleages petered out. At first, the rage focused on serious offenses—rape, pillaging, and so forth—but, as with the medieval beef, the condemnations soon piled up over minutiae that previously only mattered to scholars and historical fiction writers.

Thus creatine, a performance-enhancing aid that continues to be legal (if rarely used anymore, like many supplements because of the Darkside History movement), took on the same retroactive stigma as anabolic drugs that are actually dangerous and illegal. For the ancient Egyptian pyramid builders, this meant that they must take their place in the #ancienthallofshame, along with the Chinese military, Aztec games judges, and Mayan executioners (who, according to one outrager on Twitter, "regarded their bodies as temples more than their temples as temples").

Like medieval outrage, antiquity outrage will wear itself out Googling every example of a line being crossed at the dawn of recorded human history. But for now, millions of people who probably slept through world history class are bonding over the shaming of early civilizations, and not only for big-time barbarities, but also for supposedly giving themselves an assist in construction projects, large-scale battles, and ritualistic contests.

In light of #darksidehistory's viral status, you would be wise not to challenge the "ancient Egypt cheated" argument for fear of denunciation. Egypt's own Egyptological Research Society took some lashes from the #darksidehistory cane recently when it published a blog post pointing out two salient facts about creatine. Citing numerous references, the researchers pointed out that Michel Eugène Chevreul extracted the compound from meat in 1832 (the word creatine comes from *kreas*, the Greek word for flesh) and that Alfred Chanutin confirmed its muscle-building effect in 1926.

Not only did outragers bully the staff of three retired professors into deleting the blog post, they explained away a sizable technical problem and rewrote history when one #darksidehistorian tweeted:

"Of couse [sic] we can't confirm the invention of ancient performance-enhancing aids. The ancients kept no records of them because they knew they'd get called out by a #pureandnatural society that is way smarter than them since we're thousands of years in the future."

239,422 retweets after that deadly blow to fact-checking, Chevreul and Chanutin took a slight loss in distinction when they became the scientists who "rediscovered" what the Egyptians (who were at least smart enough to invent an early form of toothpaste) knew about creatine, but left off the records, over two thousand years earlier.

But even if we all agree that evil performance-enhancing drugs and supplements were available and in use in the ancient world, the question remains: How far do we extend our definition of #ancientcheating? To date, no one has offered a coherent, comprehensive answer within the Darkside History movement.

Some outragers accuse the ancient Egyptian pyramid builders of #frictioncheating because they poured water on the sand in front of the sledges they used to transport the stones to the work site (a trick left off the papyrus scrolls, much like performance-enhancing aids). Others castigate them for having used ramps to #cheathaul the blocks up the monument-in-progress (another shortcut omitted from government records). Some—vegans and nonvegans—even pillory the labor force for having consumed thousands of pounds of meat daily to #darkfuel their long hours in the desert heat. Apparently, the workers were supposed to restrict protein intake, an act that would resonate with the New Ascetic movement within many fitness communities.

The future is not looking bright for the dim past.

Antiquity outrage has penetrated public consciousness so deeply that many people who are probably not losing sleep over the Giza pyramid builders' meat consumption will also retweet or repost the latest #darksidehistory meme to show they too take pride in being #pureandnatural. Understandably, they want to side with what is right and decent, and if all you have to do is share a cartoon depicting a tub of creatine on a scale outweighing the feather of *Maat*, the ancient Egyptian goddess of truth, so be it. This is how social media users all over the world show up as good citizens in the age of computer-phones.

Speaking of phones, it would be an interesting experiment if we could travel back to the disgraced period of the week and still have free Wi-Fi. Would we post a wisecrack about the buff Egyptian pyramid builder who risks life and limb in hopes that a deceased person of privilege can ride a boat into the next life? Or would we come to his aid, regardless of how we feel about his supplement problem and religious beliefs? And if we did work up a sweat beside the big, deluded lug, would we eschew the ancient lunchwagon with its protein-rich menu of cattle, goat, and sheep meat? And while we're at it, might we grow curious as to what this crazy pyramid project is about?

A Google search—the outrager's closest friend after the share button—will show us we have more in common with the ancient Egyptians than the Darkside History movement wants us to believe.

The pyramids were constructed as a tomb for the late pharaoh and as a launching point for his journey to the underworld. After the funerary rites were observed inside the burial chamber, the pharaoh's soul was conducted to the Hall of Truth for judgment by Osiris, god of the dead, and his conferees known as the Forty-two Judges. The pharaoh was then called upon to recite the sins he did not perform in life and to have his heart weighed on a scale against the aforementioned feather. If his heart weighed less than the feather, the pharaoh proceeded to eternal life. If his heart outweighed the feather, his soul was destroyed and his heart eaten by a monster.

One can imagine Osiris's social media producer breaking the bad news to the people: "The late king did not live according to the will of the gods. #nowyoureallydie #byee #truth #halloftruth #pharaohfail #notinmykingdom #istandbythegods."

The problem with antiquity outrage, and outrage in general, is that anyone with Internet access can administer the Judgment of Osiris. With a scroll or click, we can review a person, thing, or idea and weigh it against a feather that stands for whatever truth we decide reflects "the will of the gods" at the time. Unfortunately, our gods are not archetypes of humanity's soul-tending needs, but the craving to be justified and the power to project our inflexible notions of moral hygiene onto anyone and anything (including the ghosts of old civilizations) that fails to reinforce our group narratives of who we are and what we value.

The Darkside History movement took the ethical complexities of modern competition—not only for championship titles, but for jobs, scholarships, artistic placements, even social media attention—and, for lack of a healthier outlet, deified (or demonized?) them in a mythical reimagining of societies from a remote and silent past. As a result, we have developed a puritanically warped obsession with a world that preceded every comfort and convenience we depend upon to click to the next rage-a-thon. Never mind that the more we excoriate against—and rewrite—antiquity, the greater hold the past takes on the present.

So watch out, Neanderthals.

It was one thing to take a naturally occurring flame and keep it burning for heat or protection. But to fashion stone tools to make fire whenever you want it? You may be warming your hands soon in the #iceagehallofshame. Even at this writing, the outragers are building a case against prehistory. If it turns out you used modafinil (a so-called "smart pill") to expand your understanding of the combustion process, then may the gods help you.

THE LAST GLORIOUS RIDE OF EL BARKO PODEROSO

AT A QUARTER PAST TEN, STEVE WALKED TO THE STORE. HE picked up a bottle of Ibuprofen and a box of wine. Thank God people hadn't bought up all the wine. He could stretch a jar of coconut oil for a few weeks, but not his Cabernet Sauvignon.

When he stepped outside the store, the rain was falling. The man and dog in front of the newsboxes had gone. Random thought: If he told the panhandler, "I'll give you ten bucks if you use it to get your dog's nails trimmed," would the man do it? Walking home, Steve imagined the panhandler taking his dog to the crotchety lady who ran the dog salon up the street.

I need to find a new groomer, he thought, then remembered that wasn't an issue anymore.

He turned onto his street and walked along the centerline.

At first, when the street in front of his house had collapsed, he had felt pedestrians should stay on the sidewalk. But his writer mind dared him to be adventurous, and he had to admit jaywalking like an asshole made him more aware of everyday life on the block.

Nothing kills curiosity like a to-do list, though—especially one dashed off with adrenaline—so particulars like objects heaped at the sides of neighbors' houses failed to interest Steve as he thought about dog matters and laundry and returning DVD rentals.

I should have worn a hat, he thought. I'm so tired of this rain. I'm so tired.

The crowd on his lawn had gotten bigger since he had stepped out. It flowed from his front door into his driveway and up to the parking strip. At least people droned on in low tones. Still, there were so many of them —way too many after the total isolation he'd become used to for nine weeks. To delay proximity overload, he stopped at the cylindrical cement wall enclosing the sinkhole.

Twelve feet high, splattered with black, snot-like, apocalypse-stopping rain… a monument to the power of water below blighted by the power of water above. Someone had propped a pink teddy bear up beside the bottom rung of the visitors' steel ladder. Rain-soaked, it looked like pictures he had seen of birds trapped in an oil spill.

As they had done every time Steve came or went, the people in front of his house made way. He threaded through the crowd with head lowered and realized how tightly he'd been squeezing his bag handles to protect the groceries from the rain. Between his death grip on the wine and pills and his aversion to the cold, slimy rain, he was carrying a lot of muscle tension on his forty-nine-year-old frame. He was also beginning to feel paranoid.

Something about staring at people's feet distorted his auditory processing. The conversational strands he had heard before—the *what people don't gets* and *it's so stupid becauses* and *you would think it's obviouses*—took on a concerted, jeering quality that made him sweat, even though the March air felt like winter with a dash of gooey precipitation.

"I mean, if they can't figure out…" A woman said, then recognized the homeowner and turned to a man *grossly misconstruing* to someone between the porch swing and pillar.

Because he had forgotten to turn on the porch light again, Steve tried six times before he unlocked the front door.

"THEY'RE STILL out of coconut oil," Steve said.

Marie, Steve's wife, kept playing the game on her phone. She lay sideways on the fireplace surround, sprawled on the cot mattress they hadn't taken camping since their twenties. Sweatshirted, gnome-pajamaed, slipper-booted, firelight woven into her mohawk's kaleidoscopic glyphs, she looked exactly the way he had left her to go shopping.

So did El Barko Poderoso in his round, purple bed, breathing slowly in sleep or unconsciousness.

"I figured they would be," Marie said. "Oh, crap, my phone is dying. People are so stupid."

Steve snorted.

"What?" Marie said.

"Nothing. You want Ibuprofen?"

"What was so funny?"

"Nothing. Do you want Ibuprofen?"

"Not now, thanks. Hey—are you mad at me?"

"No," Steve said.

"You seem mad. Did something happen?"

"No, I'm not mad."

"Okay, fine. Are you going to write some more?"

"No, of course not."

"Well, I don't know."

Marie petted the pug/Chihuahua/Boston Terrier's head. From what Steve could tell, El Barko Poderoso had not changed position since that morning. Eyes half open, chin on the bed's curved edge, right ear standing straight against the fleece lining, barely audible puffs releasing from the worn-out thunder generator of his long-for-a-pug snout. The caress behind his ears should have stirred him.

"You should sit with us," Marie said.

"I'm going to."

Steve changed his shirt and pants and threw the sullied clothes in the wash. He took three Ibuprofen and poured a mug of wine. At thirteen minutes to midnight, he returned to the living room and pulled the rocking chair toward the fireplace. The firelog was down to a single tongue of flame.

Lying in the fetal position with eyes closed, Marie said, "We need to decide if we're going to call the vet. The price goes up after midnight."

"How much?"

"I don't remember. I'd have to look."

"I guess it doesn't matter."

"I mean, it sort of matters," Marie said.

"If someone comes here, I want them to take him away. I don't care if it's extra."

"If someone comes, we'll have them take him away. The big question is, do we want to call the vet now?"

Steve sipped his wine.

He listened to the murmurs of *miss the point* and *give up their preconceived notions* and *some people should not* on the front porch.

"Maybe it'll happen naturally," he said.

"Maybe. He's definitely working on it." Marie sniffled and stroked the dog's unresponsive head again. "Oh, El Barko Poderoso..."

"All right, let's hold off."

"You're doing good, little buddy. You're doing so good."

For a while, they watched the fire burn and El Barko Poderoso move his covers up and down with soft, shallow, un-pug-like breaths. At a little past one o'clock, Marie sat up on the cot mattress and hugged her knees to her chest, tilting her hips slightly to ease pressure off her left buttock.

"I didn't want to hold off on the vet because of the price," Steve said.

"I know, Steve."

"I wish those goddamn people out there would go to someone else's house."

"But I think it's nice that we're giving them a safe space to return to socializing."

"They've been able to socialize anywhere for the last seven days."

"I know, but people don't know how to be around each other anymore."

"They can go to Hillary and Andrew's house. Or Angus and Christina's house. Or Kevin and Rachel's house."

"Do you remember when El Barko Poderoso tried to bite off Kevin's dick?"

Steve frowned.

"I know you remember," Marie said, "I just want to talk about it. Kevin comes over and asks if he can give El

Barko Poderoso a treat. El Barko Poderoso's like, 'Oh yes, give me that treat,' and then as soon as he eats it, he jumps up and sinks his teeth in Kevin's crotch. He was literally hanging off of Kevin's big shorts."

"Like when you played tug-of-war with him," Steve said. He got up from the rocking chair. "I'm going to the kitchen, do you need anything?"

"No, thanks, I think I'm going to have cereal in a minute." Marie smiled. "Tug-of-war. Do you remember how strong the little butthead used to be with those short front legs of his? Do you remember the time he pulled me off the couch and tripped me up on the carpet?"

STEVE TURNED off the television and turned the rocking chair back toward the fireplace.

The fire had burned out, leaving the orange glow from the lamp on the mantel. Marie lay on her side, asleep. Her phone, a half-drunk glass of water, and a bowl with a spoon and crumpled paper towel in it crowded the floor space between her and El Barko Poderoso.

She had cried herself to sleep watching their unconscious dog and reminiscing. Steve had played his DVDs in the background while she talked about El Barko Poderoso's decade-and-a-half of adventures. The time he rolled around on a dead crow. The time he slipped from his leash at the beach. The time he ran over to her and peed on her foot. The time he broke out in hives when she applied a homeopathic remedy to his teeth. The time he almost choked to death from eating dinner too fast.

Steve had caught snippets of *I Eat Your Children* and *Butt Gloves Killer* while Marie told the well-told stories.

He'd had no idea what went on in either movie. He had a hard enough time following film plots without his wife telling dog anecdotes and a bunch of people in front of his house telling *erroneous assumption* and *popular misconception* anecdotes. Yet, if he had rented *I Eat Your Grandchildren* and *Butt Gloves Killer: Turn the Other Cheek,* he would have tried to stay awake through the sequels. Anything to put off what he had to do next.

Steve set his mug on the floor and went to El Barko Poderoso. He had not gone near him since yesterday afternoon. He got on both knees and frowned at the emaciated animal resting inside the bed under a brown blanket and orange bath towel. Bending down as far as he could, he kissed the flap of skin over the dog's mouth. Then the indentation between the eyes. Then the top of the apple-shaped head. Keeping his mouth against the forehead, he said, "Thank you, you're a good boy. You are so good to us."

His way of saying good night and goodbye.

El Barko Poderoso had different plans, however. Steve hadn't separated from the dry, smelly forehead when the nose that had kept him up so many nights drew a deep, ragged breath, followed by a gagging sound. Steve kissed the dog again. He couldn't tell if he felt heat from his own breathing or some last reserve of energy spending itself inside the well-worn brain case. Or both.

If he didn't know better, he would have thought El Barko Poderoso was dreaming now, quivering with the altered breathing pattern.

The inhalations grew louder and harsher and faster. Taking the white front foot from under the covers, Steve pushed his nose into the bony ridge above the dog's eye and whispered, "I love you, buddy, you're doing so good.

I love you." He felt as though they were racing toward a tunnel together, a primal, strenuous act that formed a new heart between them, one that would give only a few beats, the rhythm of canine skull bone and human nose cartilage powering the final, furious strides.

Then a congested-sounding voice said inside his head: "Raising the incline, now. Higher. Higher. Wow! Just look at those clouds. Stay with me. Up, up, we're going up toward those clouds."

Steve fought the urge to look at Marie's phone. Had an ad popped up and started playing on it?

"Keep climbing," the voice went on. "Feel the burn. We're melting some serious calories now. That's it. Don't stop. We're almost there. Climb... climb... climb!"

Now Steve drew back as his little buddy moved away from him. Stretching his neck and front leg forward, El Barko Poderoso slid over the bed and went stiff as if to see how far he could extend without falling to the floor. This is it, Steve thought. Still, the dog was not finished. Like a balloon deflating, he shrank back into the bed and lay on his side with white paw drawn close to his chin. He looked like a puppy, except for his eyes being half open and the loose skin around his neck forming a kind of puffy shirt collar.

Steve pressed his mouth to the dog's forehead again and waited.

"We did it," the voice said inside his head. "Let's take a moment and celebrate. Just look around... it's absolutely breathtaking."

He's gone, Steve thought, and sat on his heels. My little buddy—

But no, another breath. This time through the mouth,

the lips quivering, the sound wet and forced from the back of the throat.

"Nicely done," the inner voice said. "What a gorgeous way to end this mountain run."

And another breath and another breath, the mouth working hard, the half-open eyes relaxed and rolled back.

"It doesn't get any better than that," the inner voice said.

After a few moments, Steve lay his head against the dog's chest. He heard noises that sounded like indigestion to his untrained ear, but no heartbeat.

Forehead, indentation, lip, nose, paw, neck, Steve kissed them with tears. Then he straightened and trembled as he looked at his dog's body. What to do now? His adrenaline was pumping. He disconnected Marie's phone from the charger and checked the time on the lock screen: 3:39 a.m.

He pulled the dog's eyelid down, went to the kitchen and poured a mug of wine.

"HE'S ALIVE, I CHECKED," Marie said, looking at Steve cross-eyed, then lay on her side again and closed her eyes. He sat on the floor beside the deathbed and drank wine.

He looked at El Barko Poderoso lying under the covers in picture-perfect repose. He wondered about the voice that had spoken inside his head. He wanted to think El Barko Poderoso had invited him into his doggy death dream of racing up a mountain. But "raising the incline?" "Feel the burn?" Obviously, that wasn't dogspeak, even if dogs could speak. They were lines from a simulation in a mock treadmill commercial whipped up by Steve's subconscious… a bizarre form of self-soothing while he witnessed his best nonhuman friend's death.

He had anthropomorphized his pet to the very end, pretending the dog connected with him telepathically in the congested-sounding voice that he and Marie jokingly used to translate the animal's insistent barks. A ridiculous escape mechanism. But then, Steve wrote silly books and rented campy movies and called his dog El Barko Poderoso—why wouldn't his imagination script some off-kilter commentary while he observed the vigil he had dreaded for fourteen years? Occam's razor: When faced with competing theories, the simplest explanation should be taken as likeliest to be correct.

Steve set his mug down and belched. As usual, after six or seven drinks, the wine made him gassy and cruel toward himself. Only this time, his adrenaline rush had cleared his mind enough that he saw the pattern in his self-talk. Supposing his subconscious had spoken to him in his dog's voice, it could also manipulate him with the language of the people in front of his house. What did it matter if he had imagined the dog voice or experienced mystical communion with his pet—however miraculous that would be? The hardest part of loving his little buddy was over.

He belched quietly and shook his wife's knee. "Marie. Marie. Marie."

Marie stirred and propped herself on one elbow. "Hm? How's El Barko—"

"He's gone."

She craned her neck and squinted at the dead dog in the orange lamp light.

"Oh, little buddy," she said, and pulled the orange bath towel up to his neck.

"I got up to go to bed," Steve said. "I went over to him to say goodnight. I figured he would either be gone by the time I got up or we would have to call the vet. I told him thank you and he was a good boy."

"Aw," Marie said, and smiled.

"Then his breathing changed." Steve sniffed back tears. "It sounded like he was reverse sneezing. I kept telling him that he was doing good and I loved him. Then he went stiff. I thought he might fall out of the bed, but he relaxed and took a few more breaths. They—" Steve didn't know what to say next.

Marie took his hand. "You know those breaths don't mean he was suffering."

"I know."

"Such a good boy, El Barko Poderoso."

"Are you mad that I didn't wake you before it happened?"

"Of course not. I've been telling him for weeks, 'You need to tell Daddy when you're ready.' My job was to be his hospice nurse at the end… yours was to help him move on."

"So we have to wait a few hours before we can take him to the vet's?"

Marie woke her phone and looked at the time on the lock screen. "We have about six hours. You should go to bed. I'll stay down here with him."

"I can't. I don't even think I can…" Steve sighed. "I know what I want to do."

"What's that?"

He climbed to his feet, marched the kinks out of his knees and hips and looked at the strangers silhouetted in the sidelights around the front door.

"I want to go down into the sinkhole," he said.

"What?"

"I've been meaning to check it out. I feel like now's the time. I have to get out of here for a bit and I want to take El Barko Poderoso with me. I'll be back sometime before 10."

Marie scowled at him as if to say, *Why would you want to take our dead dog into a sinkhole in the middle of the night?*

"It's freezing out there," she said.

"I know."

"I can't go with you."

"I didn't think you'd be able to."

"This sucks having cancer," Marie said. "This sucks losing our dog."

Steve sighed and watched his wife cry.

Knuckling tears from her eyes, Marie said, "You should put him in a trash bag to make it easier to carry him."

"God, I can't do that."

"You're keeping him in his bed, right? How are you going to climb up and down a ladder holding him in his bed?"

"I'll make it happen."

Marie climbed to her feet. "Here. I'll get some stuff to take with you and I will put him in a bag. Think of it as a body bag, okay? You can take it off once you're down there."

"Marie, please. I have an idea. It would help if you got my phone and hat and coat and shoes while I take care of something."

"Fine." Marie sniffled and stalked into the kitchen. He listened to her march upstairs.

WHILE SHE GATHERED HIS THINGS, Steve dragged the dog

bed toward the front door. An oval stain marked the spot on the fireplace surround where El Barko Poderoso had emptied his bladder for the last time. Poor little buddy, he thought. He turned the thumb latch on the door and let in the icy March night, noting that at least the rain had stopped. Then he moved around behind the dog bed, picked it up and carried it across the threshold.

The people on the porch stared at him.

"My dog died," he said.

"Oh, boy," a man said, in front of the hanging egg chair opposite the porch swing. "I'm so sorry."

"That is a terrible, sickening feeling," another man said, on the lawn.

"What was your dog's name?" The woman closest to Steve asked, peering into the dog bed. "Aw, how adorable."

"A boy, I take it?" A man said, by the pillar on the same side as the porch swing. "He looks like he went peacefully."

"He did," Steve said. "His name was El Barko Poderoso."

"I love it," the woman bent over the bed said. "It's bold. It suits him."

"What a beautiful gift to give to your baby," another woman said, as she stepped onto the bottom porch step. "My Rudy died in my arms a year ago yesterday. Oh my gosh, this is going to make me cry. I'm sorry."

"Is there anything we can do?" The man by the hanging egg chair said.

"I want to take him down into the sinkhole and sit with him before we drive him to the vet's to be cremated."

His announcement drew frowns, nods, sighs.

Then a woman on the sidewalk waved her arms overhead. "All right, everyone. I need volunteers to get on the ladder with me outside and inside the tower. We'll form a chain and hand the dog off to each other."

"We'll make it happen," another woman said, echoing his boast to Marie, somewhere in the crowd on the lawn.

Steve watched as people streamed toward the tower and climbed the ladder. The woman who had bent over the dog bed touched his hand. He had not felt anyone but Marie's touch since the restrictions on human contact had been lifted.

"You should put him down for a minute," she said.

He set the bed on the porch and wondered what to do with his hands, though no one was looking at him anymore. The crowd had gathered before the tower and formed a semicircle spilling over onto the lawn across the street. People looked on as the volunteers lined up on alternate sides of the ladder. There were whispers, giggles.

Steve started as Marie came up beside him.

"Put these on," she said, and held out his clothes. She shivered. "Brrrr! What's all this?"

"They're handing El Barko Poderoso off to each other to get him into the sinkhole."

"Oh, wow."

"I can get him out myself if they're not here later. It's a nice gesture, though."

"It's super nice. Put your clothes on."

Steve threw on coat, hat, and shoes and took his phone from Marie. They looked at each other. For the first time in a week, they had the porch to themselves.

"Ready," a voice shouted, from inside the tower.

"Commence hand-off," a man hollered, to laughter and cheers.

The woman who had lost her dog a year ago stepped

toward the porch and held her hands out. "Come here, El Barko Poderoso."

Steve looked at Marie. "You were his mama. You should start the chain."

She choked back a sob. She lifted the dog bed and walked it to the woman on the walkway.

"It's damp on the bottom," Marie said.

The woman smiled sadly. "Of course."

Standing beside his wife, Steve watched the purple bed pass from link to link in the human chain. The sight made him think of villagers passing around a newborn. Those who took the bed tilted their heads and peered into it with smiles or tears or both. Those around them crowded in for a glimpse of the puppy El Barko Poderoso had become again in death. Eight days ago, such teamwork would have been impossible.

His urge to take his dog into a sinkhole had transformed the dead-end street into an impromptu memorial park. From their lingering looks, everyone in the chain had lost a Rudy of whatever breed, whatever species. His little buddy had given people a chance to mingle their private griefs in a commemoration of the simplest love.

It doesn't get any better than that, Steve thought, thinking of the voice he had heard inside his head.

Then up the tower El Barko Poderoso went, volunteers relaying his urine-soaked bed up the outer wall like waiters in a dream-like circus act. Riding on shadowed hands, he appeared to float over the top of the massive cylinder and descend into its mouth. Inside the tower, more helpers lowered him into his temporary crypt ten feet below street level.

"He's down," a voice shouted from inside the enclosure.

Marie squeezed Steve's hand. "I'm going inside. I'm freezing. I love you."

"I love you, too," Steve said. "I know it's weird that I want to do this."

"Be careful. I hope it doesn't start raining again."

Marie went inside the house and closed the door.

The volunteers had finished descending the ladder. Steve walked into the crowd. The condolers closed in around him, clasping his shoulders and arms and giving him messages to pass onto his dog to pass onto their dogs, cats, rabbits, pigs, and even reptiles.

This time as he moved among them, he kept his head up.

STEVE'S PHONE VIBRATED.

"Do you need anything?" Marie texted. "A pillow? Blanket?"

"I'm good," Steve texted back.

"How is it down there?"

"Okay." He started to say the whole thing had been paved over and the floor had a trench around it for the rainwater, but changed his message to say, "See you in a few." He turned off the phone and slipped it into his coat pocket.

He leaned his head against the paved wall and closed his eyes.

Here I am, at the bottom of my life, he thought.

It wasn't enough that his wife was fighting cancer. It wasn't enough that humanity had dropped any semblance of sanity during a pandemic. It wasn't enough that people still had no idea how to provide for themselves after a quarantine. His dog had died. Yes, he had been old and sick, but even dehydrated and partially paralyzed, El Barko Poderoso had kept order in his kingdom, dictating the hours with his demands and the spaces with his needs. Without his tyrannical presence, Steve and Marie would be left with a house of odd angles and warped perspectives, the perpetual 4 a.m.-fears of Marie's life-threatening disease in a world that had been rocked by an outbreak deadlier than any in centuries.

He drew his knees toward his chest and hugged himself.

Staring into the darkness, Steve realized the sinkhole was a perfect place to meditate. He had tried meditation a few times during the strictest days of the quarantine. Grounding himself was no substitution for wine, of course… but here he was, in a natural isolation booth, the Cabernet wearing off and indignation sparking in its place. He might as well try and center his mind since this was the last time he would spend alone with his little buddy.

Steve squirmed around, getting as comfortable as he could with no lumbar support and his sitz bones resting on the trench drain's edge. He drew a few belly breaths. His heart pounded as he recalled El Barko Poderoso's last breaths.

He stopped, touched the body beside him, closed his eyes and started belly breathing again. He imagined his sorrow in liquid form. Black, oozy, yet healing, like the rain that had stopped the pandemic. He pictured the sadness flowing out of him, running into the trench drain.

His breathing slowed.

HE WAS THINKING of his to-do list when a disk rimmed with flashing red lights descended inside the tower.

It measured half the diameter of the shaft. It looked metallic and made a low droning noise. Past the halfway point, a man and woman became visible on its upper surface, illuminated by a broad beam of white light coming from the floor. They were tall, gaunt, and pale, dressed in tight, turquoise jumpsuits and wearing gold medallions around their necks. The man had dark, curly hair and the woman had blonde, straight hair that fell past her shoulders. They stood behind consoles mounted on helical stands, oblivious of Steve or ignoring him.

The hovercraft stopped two feet above the floor of the sinkhole. The man floated to the dog bed, picked it up and glided back to the disk. Steve tried to object, but he couldn't move. Heart slamming against his rib cage, he watched the man place the bed at waist height above the center of the disk and return to his console. The bed levitated in the white light shooting from the floor.

Steve's eyes filled with tears. The woman looked at him and tapped her medallion. At its center, an oval lit up. The green light soothed him. The woman then glanced back at the bed and nodded. The bed rotated a few degrees and tilted so El Barko Poderoso's white paw came into view.

Steve watched the disk take off, red lights flashing, then disappear into the night sky.

BRIGHT LIGHT.

Blue sky.

Stabbing pain in his neck.

Steve blinked until his vision cleared, then struggled to his feet.

The dog bed was gone.

He turned on his phone. Marie had texted him.

"We decided to let you sleep. They brought El Barko Poderoso back up for you and put him in the car."

He texted back: "Be up soon."

He looked at the wet spot where the bed had been.

Funny.

He really had hoped he'd seen El Barko Poderoso being whisked away by angels in the guise of space people. For a minute, before reading Marie's text, he had allowed himself to believe in extraterrestrial visitors who looked like white people dressed up for a futuristic-themed party at a Seventies disco club. He had not wanted to consider that he might have fallen asleep and fulfilled a spiritual fantasy for his dog derived from memories of television shows he'd watched as a child.

Then again, why couldn't his little buddy have comforted him through a shared dream, as he might also have done when he took his last breaths? Dogs had been known to find their owners from faraway places.

Sentimental, to be sure, and probably riddled with fallacies, but even the people in front his house could stop debunking now and then and grieve without criticism, without reduction.

Interpretation aside, Steve would always think of El Barko Poderoso's white paw before his guides transported him to parts unknown.

He moved his arms in circles and stretched his neck. Gritting his teeth, he looked at the steel ladder trailing twenty-two feet up the cement wall. He was so tired, and yet there was so much to do. Take the body to the vet's.

Return the DVDs. Find coconut oil. Start the laundry. And the CT scan next week. For Steve and Marie, the fear of spread didn't end with a deluge of sludgy rain. The dread and isolation continued.

Thank God the people had taken the dog bed up. Steve grabbed onto the ladder and set his foot on the bottom rung. This was going to be awful, he thought.

Then he remembered the voice that had sung the song of a dying king:

"We're melting some serious calories now. Climb… climb… climb!"

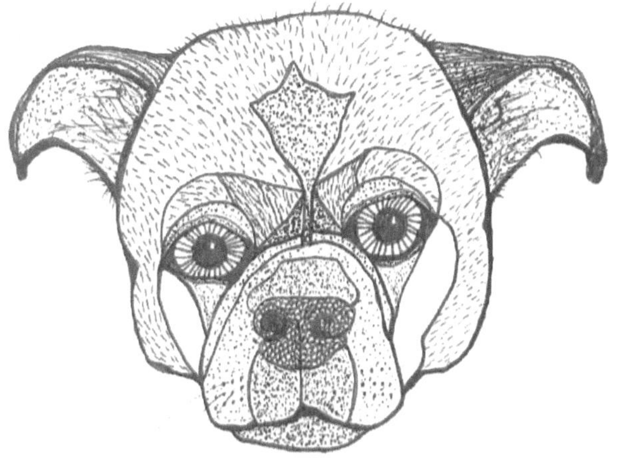

MY HOPE FOR THE SCARIEST HORROR NOVEL

The scariest
horror novel
I will ever read

has phrases like
"enlarged lymph
nodes"
and
"concerning for
metastasis"

and a protagonist
who happens
to be my wife

and chapters
that come out
each week

and an ending
to be written

by Western
and Eastern
medicine

and the protagonist
herself
of course

I wouldn't buy
this novel on Amazon
but now that I'm
forced to read it

it's so visceral
and enlightening

I have such
empathy for the
characters

even the monster
is just a cluster
of frightened cells

(*calm down, Mr. Boogeyman*)

anyhow

may love prevail
in this horror novel

that is making me
become a better reader

and may all the
good people
survive

ABOUT THE STORIES

"Air Guitar Poem That Never Once Mentions Bon Jovi"—I wrote this shortly after Kara was diagnosed with cancer. It was a way to cope with my guilt-ridden sense that we might have avoided this ordeal if we had made different life choices. At least at the beginning, there was something about the oncology consultations that made me feel like a child who has done something stupid and harmful.

"Slippery When Metastasized"—Navigating a hospital can not only be distressing, it can be downright surreal. The maze of clinics, the red tape, not to mention the dizzying conversations with a specialist who can't seem to decide how to talk to you about the course of treatment… This story began as a parody of apocalyptic surgeons and grew into a tale of friendship, resilience, and reciting your birth date over and over.

"No One Understands *Rocky V* (Truth Cancer!): If you want to impress followers on your online social networks, refer to an opinion that is making the Internet rounds, shoot it down with an argument that is supposed to pass for deductive reasoning and season it with curse words and references to famous philosophers. Boom!

"Naked Liam Neeson Gets WOKE"—As I mentioned in the introduction, this story began as a joke in a hotel room at KillerCon. A debt of gratitude to my dad's suspense novels, the work of writer Douglas Hackle (whose characters include a drum fill from a Phil Collins song), and body horror maestro Brendan Vidito for the corrosive semen idea. And I don't think sex trafficking is funny, okay? But only sex traffickers would mutilate victims to create a real surgical nightmare for a torture porn film called *Human Snout Beetle*.

"Before the Def Leppard *Pyromania* Virus Destroyed Us"— I've tried to write a story about spam verbiage off and on for years. Finally, the right idea sparked and I cranked out this little pandemic story two years before COVID-19.

"Hi, It's Wolfman"—About a year ago, I watched this documentary called *Room 237*. It's about film fans who are obsessed with Stanley Kubrick's *The Shining*. Thanks to technology, they are able to dissect the film frame by frame and construct elaborate and sometimes paranoid readings of its imagery. Of course, given our reductionist age, these people were ridiculed by viewers of the documentary. Their interpretations were regarded as symptomatic and preposterous. There is truth to that, but the conspiracy theories were also charged with imagination (if not originality in every case) and driven by a pressure to unveil the hidden that people who only live in a world of facts and logic cannot know. That pressure bears down from the shadow self that dominates these wildly biased interpretations of Kubrick's film. Granted, totally giving in to the shadow self isn't healthy, as we might infer from the documentary, but working with the shadow self can have some cathartic benefits. With "Hi, It's Wolfman," I let my shadow self build a reading of *Top Gun* driven by the need for someone in my life to bear witness to my crisis, like Wolfman. Shadows are great at creating archetypes from whatever strikes their fancy. They're not sophisticated and they're not snobs. Crisis... as the spouse of a cancer patient, I often find myself wanting someone to acknowledge how terrified, exhausted, miserable, sorrowful, and angry I feel, because I mostly refrain from venting to friends who are already concerned about us or on the usual social (media) outlets to avoid making our lives even messier and more stressful. But this witness wouldn't be an actual person, which can get complicated—more like the hypothetical audience of a diary. An imaginary intimate who quietly bears witness to the work I must do, as I quietly bear witness to the work my wife must do... and who therefore knows my experience. So yeah, Tony Scott made *Top Gun* just for me. It's all there in the volleyball scene.

"Smoke Nurse"—I wrote obituaries for seven years, including my dad's. I had no illusions about my mortality. Close to my office, there was a certain skyscraper I wouldn't walk by because I kept picturing someone jumping off it and taking me out with them. Through the thousands of obituaries I wrote, and the phone calls I made to the legions of mourners, I developed a practical and dutiful awareness of what Americans tend to think of as morbid and macabre. Anyway, I heard somewhere about music-thanatologists—people who use harp and voice to comfort patients who are actively dying. The idea of an outside party adding a soothing influence to the experience of someone leaving the world really moved me. When I wrote this story in 2009, I had no idea I would later hold my mom's hand while she was dying or my dog's paw while he was dying. Maybe a part of me did though, because when I reread this story recently it felt like 2009 me was speaking to 2020 me through Mara.

"The Third Punic War Was Not Science-Based (Truth Cancer!)"—I'm a big fan of *Kentucky Fried Movie*. It's nothing but sketches parodying anything from kung fu movies to news broadcasts to television commercials. I like how the short spoofs thread throughout the film, and that's what I wanted with the "Truth Cancer" commentaries.

"The Time I Took Hamlet Right into the Danger Zone"— This was the first story I wrote after Kara's diagnosis. The idea came about when my friend James (whose essay I quoted from in the introduction) invited me to give a humorous presentation with him at an academic motor-cycle conference. The International Journal of Motorcycle Studies organizers were kind enough to let me read this to attendees, even though I don't know a thing about motorcycles.

"Jim Morrison Library Poem"—I wrote this for an event that took place at a bar during the 2019 AWP Conference in Portland, Oregon. Three small presses—including CLASH Books, who released my second collection, *This Is a Horror Book*—competed to see who could write the best poem inspired by a song, read the poem before an audience and then sing the song karaoke-style. Thanks to Christoph Paul and Leza Cantoral for letting me creep out the AWP audience with my ode to "People Are Strange."

"Ding-Dong-Ditch"—Chronologically, the second of three stories I wrote in a five-year period about someone helping someone else die.

"Insidious in the Month of June"—And this is the first story. Nurse Judith is an extreme example of what happens when you realize you can't make someone put forth positive effort for their health. You feel the sting of disappointment at first, and then you get pissed. And if you're telepathic, you become a vengeful god.

"The Necromancer's Guide to Positive Self-Talk"—Like "Naked Liam Neeson Gets WOKE," this story came about from a conversation with the Freddy's Crew. Originally, I had no plans to work a *Star Wars* angle into the story. But I couldn't resist when I realized the War Moon was a kind of misnomer in the magical world of the Whispering Gunslinger. Once I put in Old Ben's quote from the first *Star Wars* movie, I knew my narrator had to be excitable and intrusive. He's like the kid who has to tell you everything that happens in a movie he watched the night before, but can't help work in references to another movie he's obsessed with. For the most part, this story is a playground mash-up of *High Plains Drifter* and *Return of the Jedi*, if you hadn't already guessed.

"We Are Osiris and the Forty-Two Judges (Truth

Cancer!)"—This started as another parody and morphed into a mock thinkpiece that makes a lot of sense to me. Maybe the satire gets old, I don't know, but I had a lot of fun writing it. And I learned a lot about the Giza pyramids and creatine monohydrate.

"The Last Glorious Ride of El Barko Poderoso"—This one's for my little buddy… Iggy Sancho died on March 15, 2020, just three months and five days shy of his sixteenth birthday. He left me to mourn him in the midst of unemployment, cancer worries and duties, absolute cluelessness about what I want to do with my life, and the madness of a global outbreak. To help me cope, I wrote this story. I wanted a protagonist who expressed my state of mind and the woes of living the jobless, locked-down, freaked-out life months before the world got caught up in a quarantine. I wanted a character who felt dead inside and cut off from those around him even before he loses his dog. I also wanted to imagine people apart from their rotten online personas and connected through love of their furry companions. This story makes fifteen for the years my little buddy barked and marked his way through the terrestrial realm.

"My Hope for the Scariest Horror Novel"—Now that I think about it, this is for the caregivers/supporters who are deeply invested in their special someone's struggle to get past cancer. Not everyone in our position rises to the occasion. Some quit the relationship, some lash out at their already beleaguered partner and some refuse to perform the unsexy services that a cancer patient may at times require outside of the hospital. As a true supporter, you get under the yoke and carry it for as long as you must, wondering if it will ever end and hating that there is a whole world out there that knows nothing of what you're going through. That has been my experience so far, anyway. I hope it changes for the better. I hope all the right people survive.

ABOUT THE AUTHOR

The author and his wife, Kara "Picante" Muir, in a Mad Max-inspired photo shoot.

Photo courtesy of Lenny Gotter.

Charles Austin Muir is the author of the Splatterpunk Award-nominated comedic horror collection, *This Is a Horror Book*, and the not-nominated-for-anything bizarro collection, *Bodybuilding Spider Rangers and Other Stories*.

Since his first publication in 2005, he has had stories appear in magazines and anthologies throughout the U.S. and U.K., and has snuck into books alongside such horror greats as Graham Masterton and Ray Garton. His story "Ding-Dong-Ditch" received an honorable mention in the Twenty-first Edition of *The Year's Best Fantasy and Horror*. His weirder fiction draws on literary influences such as Douglas Hackle and D. Harlan Wilson, childhood obsessions such as *Star Wars* and *The Bionic Woman*, and an interest in strength that led him to become a competitive powerlifter and later a personal trainer. He lives in Portland, Oregon, with his pugs and pit-lab mix and Kara "Picante," artist, massage therapist, performer, and 2019's fourth best air guitarist in the U.S. (in a tie), not to mention the most bionic, badass partner he could have chosen to help him seek adventure and battle the forces of darkness.

www.worldsofcharlesaustinmuir.com